S0-AFP-431

How

Do

You

Live?

How

Do

You

Live?

**GENZABURO
YOSHINO**

With a foreword
by Neil Gaiman

RIDER

Rider, an imprint of Ebury Publishing,
20 Vauxhall Bridge Road,
London SW1V 2SA

Rider is part of the Penguin Random House group of companies
whose addresses can be found at global.penguinrandomhouse.com

Penguin
Random House
UK

KIMITACHI WA DOU IKIRU KA
by Genzaburo Yoshino

Text copyright © 1937, 1982 by Gentaro Yoshino

Originally published in 1982 by Iwanami Shoten, Publishers, Tokyo.

This English edition published in 2021 by Rider Books, an imprint of
Random House Group Limited, London by arrangement with the copyright
holder c/o Iwanami Shoten, Publishers, Tokyo through Japan UNI Agency, Inc.,
Tokyo. c/o Curtis Brown Ltd, NY.

Gentaro Yoshino has asserted his right to be identified as the author of this
Work in accordance with the Copyright, Designs and Patents Act 1988

Published in the United States by Algonquin Young Readers, an imprint of
Algonquin Books of Chapel Hill, a division of Workman Publishing

Translation © 2021 by Bruno Navasky
Foreword © 2021 by Neil Gaiman

www.penguin.co.uk

A CIP catalogue record for this book is available from the British Library

ISBN 9781846046452

Printed and bound in Great Britain by Clays Ltd, Elcograf S.p.A.

The authorised representative in the EEA is Penguin Random House Ireland,
Morrison Chambers, 32 Nassau Street, Dublin D02 YH68.

MIX
Paper from
responsible sources
FSC® C018179

Penguin Random House is committed to a sustainable
future for our business, our readers and our planet. This book
is made from Forest Stewardship Council® certified paper.

Foreword

This is such a strange book, and such a wise book. I wish I had been given it as a small boy, but I suspect I would have found it puzzling or even dull: a book-length essay about how we live our lives, interrupted by the story of a pre-war schoolboy in Japan dealing with friendship and bullying; or a story about growing up, bravery, cowardice, social class and finding out who you are, interrupted by essays about scientific thought and personal ethics. Sometimes the joy of books that seem to contain opposing elements is realising that without both things, you would have a lesser book. (There's a book called *Moby-Dick* by Herman Melville that contains a story about a doomed hunt for a white whale and also contains essays about whales and whale hunting. Some people like one part of the story, and some like the other. For me, the joy is that the book contains both parts, pulling at each other, each informing the other side, and that if you removed either part you would have a less interesting book.)

I read *How Do You Live?* now, in this sparkling new translation, because Hayao Miyazaki is basing his next film on it. It's a film he has said that he is making for his grandson, as a gift to the future.

The finest time I spent with Mr Miyazaki was in the building he was making for the children of the neighborhood around Studio Ghibli, where he makes his cartoons. It was built of wood, and there was a bridge across it, inside, too small for adults to cross, but the perfect size for children to go exploring. It was a space for the whole person.

Miyazaki makes films for whole people and makes films about consequences. When I worked on the English-language script of his film *Princess Mononoke*, I was astonished when I finally realised that everything in the film was about consequences of acts and actions: seemingly unrelated events are actually the consequences of other events or actions, and everyone in the film is acting according to what they believe to be their best interests without realising that what they do affects everyone else.

In *How Do You Live?*, Copper, our hero, and his uncle are our guides in science, in ethics, in thinking. And on the way they take us, through a school story set in Japan in 1937, to the heart of the questions we need to ask ourselves about the way we live our lives. We will experience betrayal and learn about how to make tofu. We will examine fear, and how we cannot always live up to who we think we are, and we learn about shame, and how to deal with it. We will learn about gravity and about cities, and most of all, we will learn to think about things—to, as the writer Theodore Sturgeon put it, *ask the next question.*

Books like this are important. I'm so glad Mr Miyazaki is making his film, not least because it means that, eighty-four years after it was written, Genzaburō Yoshino's novel can be read in English, in Bruno Navasky's gentle and winning translation, and that I got to read it.

Neil Gaiman

Introduction

Copper is in his second year of junior high school.

His real name is Honda Jun'ichi. Copper is his nickname. He's fifteen, but on the small side for fifteen, and to be honest, Copper himself is pretty sensitive about that.

At the beginning of each term, the gym teacher has the class form a line, remove their hats, and arrange themselves by height. Copper quietly slips the heel of his shoe onto a stone and cranes his neck in a painful effort to move ahead in the order somehow, but he never does. Instead he always ends up wrestling with his classmate Kitami—nicknamed Gatchin—in a fierce contest for second or third place. Of course, that's from the back end of the line.

But when it comes to grades, it's the other way around. Copper is generally first or second in the class and has hardly ever dropped to third. That said, Copper is no grade-grubber, but rather somebody who likes to play more than most. In baseball he's considered the class athlete. It's charming to see little Copper with his big glove, guarding second base. Small as he is, he's no power hitter, but he knows how to bunt, so he's always picked to bat second in the lineup.

Although he's first or second in grades, Copper has never been the class leader. It's not because he's not well liked, but rather that he can be a bit too mischievous. It wouldn't be right to make Copper the class leader, would it, when he seems happy to spend ethics class hidden from the teacher, making two rhinoceros beetles play tug-of-war, tied together by a thread? When the time comes for a parent-teacher conference, the words that his homeroom teacher says to his mother are always the same: "There's not much to be said about his studies. His test scores are exceptionally good, and as usual it seemed he would be chosen as the class leader. But . . ."

When this "But . . ." comes out, his mother thinks, *Again?* Because what comes next, invariably, is a story of Copper's mischief landing him in trouble.

Actually, Copper's mother may be partially responsible for this. When she comes home from the parent-teacher conference, she often tells him, "We had another warning from your teacher, you know," but she's not particularly severe about it. To tell the truth, his mother can't give him a hard time about this sort of thing.

The reason she can't is mostly because Copper's mischief is rarely irritating or troublesome to anyone, and he's not bad-spirited, but simply an innocent soul who makes people laugh and amuses them. But besides that, there's one more big reason: Copper has no father.

Copper's father passed away just about two years ago. He was a director at a big bank, and after he died, Copper's family moved from their mansion in the old city to a modest house in the suburbs. They let go of a number of people who worked for them, too, so aside from Copper and his mother, there were just the nanny and one maid, and it became a household of four in all. Unlike the days when his father was alive, they received few visitors, and it suddenly began to feel lonely inside the house. His mother's primary concern at that time was to preserve Copper's natural high spirits, so she found herself unable to reprimand Copper very harshly for small matters.

After they moved to the suburbs, an uncle who lived in the neighborhood would come to visit now and again. That uncle was Copper's mother's little brother, fresh out of the university with a law degree. Copper would often go to his uncle's house to play as well. The two of them were terribly close. People in the neighborhood would often see little Copper and his taller-than-average uncle walking side by side, or in the fields together playing catch, just the two of them.

Copper's nickname was first coined by this uncle. Then one Sunday, just when a schoolmate, Mizutani, had come to the house to play, the uncle dropped by as well. "Copper, Copper" was thrown about, and after that the name quickly spread to school.

Mizutani came to school and jabbered, "Hey, you know Honda, right? Well, at home he's called Copper!" And so it was that his schoolmates came to call him that. Now even his mother will sometimes address him as "Mister Copper."

Why "Copper"? Not one of his friends knows. They just think it's fun, and they all call him that without knowing why. If they ask him "Why are you called Copper?" he just laughs and never explains. But he gets a sort of pleased look on his face, so his friends want to know the reason all the more.

And on this point, we all feel no differently than his friends. So first let's start with the story of Copper's nickname. And then let's report on the curious happenings inside Copper's head.

Why such a report? Read on, and you will understand.

Chapter One

A Strange Experience

It happened one October afternoon last year, when Copper was still a first-year student. He was with his uncle, the two of them standing on the roof of a department store in the Ginza district of Tokyo.

A fine mist fell quietly and ceaselessly from the ashen sky, so that it was hard to tell if it was raining or not, and before they knew it, small silver droplets had fastened everywhere on Copper's jacket and his uncle's raincoat, and they looked as if they had been covered with frost. Copper was silent, gazing down at the Ginza Boulevard immediately below.

From seven stories up, the Ginza was a narrow channel. At the bottom, cars streamed past in great numbers, one after another. From Nihonbashi on the right side, flowing beneath him to Shinbashi on the left, and from there in the opposite direction, from the left side back to Nihonbashi, the twin currents slipped past each other, waxing and waning as they went. Here and there between the two streams, a trolley crawled sluggishly by, looking somehow world-weary. The trolleys looked as small as toys, and their roofs were slick with rain. The cars, too, and the asphalt road surface and even the trees lining the road and all else that was there were dripping wet and gleaming with the brightness of daylight shining from who knew where.

Gazing down in silence, Copper began to imagine that the individual cars were insects. *If they were bugs*, he thought, *they would be rhinoceros beetles. They're a swarm of rhinoceros beetles that comes crawling in a big hurry. Then once they've done their job, they go hurrying home. There's no knowing what it's about, but to them great affairs are happening, make no mistake.*

As Copper thought about the beetles, he noticed how the Ginza gradually narrowed in the distance, finally bending to the left, and there, where it vanished amid the tall buildings near Kyōbashi, didn't it seem like the entrance to their nest? *The little creatures, in their rush to return, disappear over there, one by one. And as they do, their replacements come hurrying back, one by one. A black one, a black one, again a black one, now a blue one, a gray one . . .*

The powdery mist continued to fall quietly as before. While immersed in his strange fantasy, Copper gazed for some time toward the Kyōbashi neighborhood and eventually raised his face. Below him, the rain-soaked streets of Tokyo spread boundlessly in all directions.

It was a dark, lonely, endless prospect, and watching it, Copper began to feel gloomy, too. As far as the eye could see, the innumerable little roofs continued, all the while reflecting the light of the leaden sky. Breaking up the flat house rows, clusters of high-rise buildings poked up here and there. The farthest of these were gradually caught up in a haze of rain and at last became silhouettes floating between the sky and the vague dullness of the mono-chrome mist. How profoundly damp it must have been! Everything was wet through and through, and it seemed that even the rocks themselves were permeated with water. Tokyo was submerged, motionless at the bottom of the cold and damp.

Copper had been born and raised in Tokyo, but this was the first time he had ever seen the streets of Tokyo show such a sad and somber face. The hustle and bustle of the city came welling up endlessly from the depths of the heavy wet air to the seventh-floor rooftop, but whether this registered in his ears or not, Copper just stood there, transfixed. For some reason, he had become utterly unable to look away. At that moment, something began to happen deep inside him, a change unlike anything that had happened to him before.

Actually, this change in Copper's heart is related to the story of how he got his nickname.

What happened first was that Copper saw, floating before him, the rain-beaten, dark winter sea.

That image may have come back to him from memories of a time Copper went with his father to the Izu Peninsula on a winter holiday. As he watched the streets of Tokyo spreading far away into the mist, the city beneath him came to seem like a vast expanse of ocean, and the buildings standing here and there looked like crags jutting up from its surface. Above the ocean, the sky hung down, threateningly low.

Copper, lost in the grip of his imagination, thought vaguely that there must be human beings living at the bottom of this ocean.

But when he came to, for some reason, Copper shivered. Those little roofs packing the earth just like sardines— under those innumerable roofs were any number of human beings! While that was a natural thing, at the same time, when he thought it over, it gave him a sort of scary feeling.

Right now, beneath Copper's very eyes, as well as in places he couldn't even see, some hundreds of thousands of people were living. How many different sorts of people were there? What were they all doing now, while Copper watched from above? What were they thinking? It was an unpredictable and chaotic world. The elderly in their eyeglasses, little girls with bobbed hair, young women with their hair done up, shopkeepers in aprons, office workers in their Western clothes—all manner of people were at once materializing before Copper's eyes and again disappearing.

"Uncle—" Copper started to speak. "I wonder how many people there are just in the places we can see from here."

"Hmm . . ." said his uncle.

"I mean, if we estimate that we can see one-tenth or maybe one-eighth of the city of Tokyo from here, then wouldn't the number of people be one-tenth to one-eighth of the population of Tokyo?"

"Well, it's not quite that simple," Copper's uncle replied, laughing. "If Tokyo's population were an average, even distribution everywhere you went, that would be correct—just as you say. But in actuality, there will be areas of heavy population density and, consequently, light areas as well, you see? So you ought to give proportional weight to these areas in your calculations. And what's more, you have daytime and nighttime—the number of people will vary immensely, you know."

"Day and night? Why would it vary?"

"Just think about it and you'll see. You and I live outside of Tokyo, don't we? But at the moment, here we are, at the very center of the city. And then when evening falls, won't we go back home? There must be any number of other people like that."

Copper mulled this over.

"Today is a Sunday," his uncle continued, "but if it were a normal weekday, look at all the places you can survey from here—Kyōbashi, Nihonbashi, Kanda, Hongo. Every morning, from outside Tokyo, immense numbers of people come charging in. And then when evening comes, they pull out again, all at once. You know yourself how crowded the commuter trains and city trolleys and buses are during rush hour."

I should have thought of that, Copper said to himself.

His uncle went on. "I suppose, to hazard a guess, one could say that there are some hundreds of thousands—no, maybe even, say, more than one million people—flowing in and out, rising and falling like an ocean tide, hmm?"

Above the two of them in their conversation, the misty rain continued to fall. Copper and his uncle stood awhile in silence, gazing at the city of Tokyo laid out below them. Beyond the falling rain, shimmering and trembling, the darkened city streets continued to run off to places unknown, where not a single human figure could be seen.

Yet below them, without a shadow of a doubt, hundreds of thousands, maybe even millions of people were thinking their own thoughts, doing their own things, and living their lives. Yes, and those people, every morning, every evening, were rising and falling like the tides.

Copper felt as if he were drifting into a big whirlpool.

"Hey, Uncle—"

"Yes?"

"People are . . ." Starting to speak, Copper turned a bit red. But he pulled himself together and spoke. "People are . . . Well, they seem a little like water molecules, don't you think so?"

"Indeed. If you are comparing human society to oceans and rivers, individual human beings could certainly be considered to be their molecules."

"And, Uncle, you're a molecule, too, aren't you?"

"That's right. And you are, too. An extra-small molecule, in fact."

"Don't make fun of me! Molecules are automatically small, aren't they? Uncle, you're too long and thin to be a molecule!"

While he was speaking, Copper looked down at the Ginza Boulevard just beneath them. Cars, cars, cars . . . Come to think of it, inside each one of those rhinoceros-beetle cars, there was, of course, a human being.

By chance, Copper's gaze settled on a single bicycle running along in the stream of automobiles. The man riding it was clearly still quite young. His billowing raincoat was wet and shiny. The young man was looking to the sides, looking back, noting with care a car that had passed him, the whole time pedaling with all his might. He sped along the asphalt road so slippery with rain, avoiding the cars to the right and left, all the while not dreaming that Copper was looking down at him from this high up.

Just then, a gray car appeared out of nowhere, overtaking two or three cars in front of it.

Look out! Up on the rooftop, Copper shouted in his heart. Any moment, he thought, the bicycle would be sent flying. Yet the young man below him swerved nimbly and let the car pass him by. Then in an instant, he had barely righted the tilting bicycle before he was off again, pedaling with all his might. The intense effort set his whole body in motion as he bore down on the pedals, one leg after the other.

Was he a messenger from somewhere, running off on some errand? Of course, Copper couldn't know. Here he was, observing this unseeing, unknowing young man from afar. And the object of his observation was totally unaware. To Copper, it was somehow a strange feeling. The place where the young man was riding was a spot that Copper and his uncle had driven past earlier that day, when they came to the Ginza.

"Uncle, when we drove by down there," Copper said, pointing below, "someone could have been watching from this rooftop."

"Yes, that's true. That is, we can't know for sure. In fact, there could be someone right now, perhaps, watching the two of us from a window somewhere!"

Copper looked around at the nearby buildings. Which building, which building? There were so many windows. At his uncle's words, all the windows seemed to face in Copper's direction as he looked. But the windows just reflected the hazy brightness outdoors, each and every one, and shone like mica. Whether people were inside and could see them, he couldn't know.

Still, Copper couldn't help feeling that somewhere unbeknownst to him, there were eyes watching him steadily. He even had the distinct impression that he could see his own figure reflected in those eyes—on a seven-story building in the hazy gray distance, a small, small figure standing on a rooftop!

Copper had an odd feeling. The watching self, the self being watched, and furthermore the self becoming conscious of all this, the self observing itself by itself, from afar, all those various selves overlapped in his heart, and suddenly he began to feel dizzy. In Copper's chest something like a wave began to pitch and roll. No, it felt as if Copper himself were pitching and rolling.

Then, in the city spreading boundless before him, the invisible tide welled up to its highest point. Before he knew it, Copper had become just another droplet inside that tide.

Staring blankly, Copper was silent for a long time.

After a while his uncle spoke. "Are you all right?"

Copper made a face like someone waking from a dream. And then, seeing his uncle's face, he gave an awkward laugh.

Several hours later, Copper and his uncle were riding in the car, headed home along the road to the suburbs. After leaving the department store, they had ducked into a theater to see a newsreel film, and then in the evening it was time to return the hired car, but by now it was completely dark. The rain continued to fall. They could see the trembling mist illuminated in the beam of the headlights.

"Before, what were you thinking?" Copper's uncle asked.

"Before?"

"On the department store rooftop. You were thinking hard about something, weren't you?"

Copper didn't know what to say. So he stayed silent. His uncle, too, after that, asked nothing. The car ran rapidly away along the pitch-dark road.

Eventually Copper spoke. "It was because I had a really strange feeling!"

"How so?"

"Well, because you were talking about the rising tide of people and the falling tide of people . . ."

His uncle made a face as if to say he didn't understand. At that, Copper spoke quickly, in a pronounced voice. "People, Uncle—they really are molecules, aren't they? Today I really started to believe that."

Under the dim light of the car, his uncle widened his eyes in surprise. Didn't Copper's face seem exceptionally lively and intense?

"Is that so?" his uncle said, and thought for a while, but presently he spoke, quietly and seriously. "Please remember that later. It's extremely important."

That evening, Copper's uncle was up late, at home in his study, writing something intently.

At times he would give his hand a rest and puff on a cigarette, then some thought would occur to him, and again he would continue to write. That went on for an hour, or perhaps an hour and a half, but at last he set down his pen and closed the notebook in which he was writing. It was a large maroon clothbound notebook.

The uncle, taking up a teacup that had been abandoned on his desk, drank down the now-cold tea in a single swallow, extended his arms in a broad stretch, and scratched his head vigorously. Then he lit a cigarette and puffed lazily for a while, but before long he opened a drawer in the desk and, tucking the notebook inside, finally turned out the light and went slowly off to bed.

Now, it will be necessary for us to take a little peek inside this notebook. Hidden inside it is the reason that Honda Jun'ichi came to be called Copper.

On Ways of Looking at Things

~~~~~~

Jun'ichi,

Today in the car when you said "Humans are really like molecules, aren't they?" you didn't realize what an earnest look you had on your face. It was truly beautiful to me. But what impressed me most deeply was not just that look. It was when I realized how seriously you were considering the question at hand that my heart was terribly moved.

For truly, just as you felt, individual people, one by one, are all single molecules in this wide world. We gather together to create the world, and what's more, we are moved by the waves of the world and thereby brought to life.

Of course, those waves of the world are themselves moved by the collective motion of individual molecules, and people can't always be compared to molecules of this or that sub-stance, and in the future, as you get older, you will come to understand this better and better. Nonetheless, to see your-self as a single molecule within the wide world—that is by no means a small discovery.

You know Copernicus and his heliocentric theory, don't you? The idea that the earth moves around the sun? Until Copernicus advanced his theory, people back then believed that the sun and the stars circled around the earth, as their own eyes told them. This was in part because, in accordance with the teachings of the Christian church, they also believed that the earth was the center of the universe. But if you think one step further, it's because human beings have a natural ten-dency to look at and think of things as if they were always at the center.

And yet Copernicus kept running up against astronomical facts that he couldn't explain this way, no matter how he tried. And after racking his brain over these in many attempts to explain them, he finally resolved to consider whether it might be the earth that circled in orbit around the sun. When he thought about it that way, all the various hitherto inexplicable matters fell into place under one neat principle.

And with the work of scholars who followed in his foot-steps, like Galileo and Kepler, this view was eventually proven correct, so that today it's generally believed to be an obvious thing. The basics of the Copernican theory—that the earth moves around the sun—are now taught even in elementary school.

But back then, as you know, it was quite a different matter: this explanation caused a terrible stir when it was first proposed. The church at the time was at the height of its power, so this theory that called into question the teachings of the church was thought to be a dangerous idea, and scholars who supported it were thrown in prison, their possessions were burned, and they were persecuted mercilessly in all sorts of ways.

The general public, of course, thought it foolish to take up such views and risk abuse for no good reason—or else to think that the safe, solid ground on which they were living was spinning off through the vast universe gave them an unsettling feeling, and they didn't care to believe it. It took some hundreds of years before there was faith enough in this theory that even elementary school students knew it, as they do today.

I'm sure you know all this from reading *How Many Things Have Human Beings Done?* but still, there may be nothing more deep-rooted and stubborn than the human tendency to look at and think of things with themselves at the center.

Whether to consider our own planet earth as just one of a number of celestial bodies moving through the universe, as

Copernicus did, or else to think of the earth as being seated firmly at the center of the universe—these two ways of thinking are not just a matter of astronomy. They inevitably circle around all our thoughts of society and human existence.

In childhood, most people don't hold the Copernican view, but instead think as if the heavens were in motion around them. Consider how children understand things. They are all wrapped up in themselves. To get to the trolley tracks, you turn left from your garden gate. To get to the mailbox, you go right. The grocer is around that corner. Shizuko's house is across the street from yours, and San-chan's place is next door. In this way, we learn to consider all sorts of things with our own homes at the center. It's similar when it comes to people as we get to know them: that one works at our father's bank; this one is a relative of my mother. So naturally, in this way, the self becomes central to our thinking.

But as we grow older, we come around to the Copernican way of thinking, more or less. We learn to understand people and all manner of things from a broader global perspective. This includes places—if I mention any region or city, you'll know it without having to reckon from your home—and people, as well: say that this is the president of such and such a bank, or this is the principal of such and such a high school, and they will know each other that way.

Still, to say that we grow up and think this way is, in fact, no more than a rough generality. Even among adults, the human tendency to think about things and form judgments with ourselves at the center remains deep-rooted.

No, when you are an adult, you will understand this. In the world at large, people who are able to free themselves from this self-centered way of thinking are truly uncommon. Above all, when one stands to gain or lose, it is exceptionally difficult to step outside of oneself and make correct judgments, and thus one could say that people who are able to think Copernicus-style even about these things are exceptionally great people. Most people slip into a self-interested way of thinking, become unable to understand the facts of the matter, and end up seeing only that which betters their own circumstances.

Still, as long as we held fast to the thought that our own planet was at the center of the universe, humanity was unable to understand the true nature of the universe—and likewise, when people judge their own affairs with only themselves at the center, they end up unable to know the true nature of society. The larger truth never reveals itself to them.

Of course, we say all the time that the sun rises and sets, and that sort of thing. And when it comes to our everyday lives, that's not much of a problem. However, in order to know the larger truths of the universe, you have to discard that way of thinking. That's true when it comes to society as well.

So that moment today—when you so deeply felt yourself

to be a single molecule within the wide, wide world—I believe that was a really big thing.

As for me, I secretly hope that today's experience will leave a deep impression on your heart. Because what you felt today, the way you were thinking your thoughts today—somehow, it holds a surprisingly deep meaning.

It represents a change to a new and broader way of thinking: the Copernican way.

~~~~~~~~~~~~~~~~~~~~~~~~~~~~~~

Some of what was written in his uncle's notebook may still be confusing, but if you read only this, I think you will understand exactly how little Jun'ichi came to be called Copper.

So that the day's experience would not be forgotten, the uncle made a point of addressing his nephew as "Copernicus" instead of "Jun'ichi." And before they knew it, that finally became "Copper."

And the fact that Copper looks sort of pleased when his friends ask him about his nickname—if you ask me, that, too, seems about right, doesn't it? He has been given the name of a truly great man, so we shouldn't expect him to feel bad about it at all.

Chapter Two

A Brave Friend

Copper may have felt like a molecule living in the wide world, but he was still a boy in his first year of junior high school. His school friends were the only ones around him, the only people he saw every day.

But this circle of friends was also a world of its own.

In this smaller world there were two people with whom Copper was particularly close. One was Mizutani—he and Copper had become friends when they were classmates in elementary school, going back and forth between each other's houses to play.

The other was Kitami, whom everyone called Gatchin.

Kitami and Copper were always shoulder to shoulder in the height lineup, as previously noted, so they had many chances to speak, but Copper hadn't liked Kitami much at first. Mizutani was slender and good-looking, was always a calm presence, and had a sort of girlish shyness, but Kitami, well, he was the complete opposite of that.

Kitami was as short as Copper, his build was as sturdy as a bulldog's, and no matter what the situation, he never held back. Whatever he was thinking, he said it quickly, without hesitation, and once he had spoken out on something, whatever it was, there was little chance he'd take it back.

"No matter what anyone says, I don't like it."

When Kitami said this, there was nothing anyone could do. This "no matter what anyone says . . ." was Kitami's trademark. He could be impossibly stubborn, so at some point some of the students had started calling him Gatchin, because it had a hard, stubborn sound.

But Gatchin was a fairly likable young man, despite his stubborn moments.

Once, on the way home from school, Copper and some friends got into an argument with Gatchin. The issue was, What sort of thing is electricity? In Kitami's view, the idea that any substance could flow through solid metal, such as inside an electrical line, was unbelievable.

So probably there was some sort of vibration being transmitted, he said, the same way light or sound worked. But Copper happened to know that an electrical current was made of electrons, which were even smaller than atoms, flowing away through the insides of the electrical lines. So he said that Kitami's view was mistaken, but Kitami wouldn't believe him at all.

"Well, you must have read it wrong. Because, number one, there isn't any space in the copper wire for the whatever to pass through, is there? It's weird! No matter what anyone says, that's impossible!"

At which point Copper had no choice but to explain the structure of matter to Kitami, letting loose his full stock of knowledge from science magazines, his extracurricular physics book, his copy of *Mysteries of the World*, and so forth: that all matter is made up of particles so small they can't be seen even with a microscope; that atoms in their turn are collections of even smaller electrons; that when we consider things as small as these, materials that we ordinarily think have no spaces or gaps at all actually are full of holes; and it's for that same reason that the small waves of X-rays are able to pierce objects that ordinary light rays can't get through.

"Is that so?" said Gatchin, still unconvinced.

At that point Copper came to a dead halt and from inside his bag removed a book that he happened to have right there on the spot, called *The Story of Electricity*, and showed the explanation of electrical currents to Kitami. This was a book written by a science professor.

"Huh," said Kitami, reading where Copper had pointed. Everyone stood still, waiting for his reply and wondering if even the stubborn Gatchin would now be forced to relent. Eventually Kitami looked up and said, "Okay, that's right. No matter what anyone says . . ."

When he started up again, everyone stared at Kitami, dumbfounded, and at that moment he followed up with "My way was totally wrong."

At this everyone heaved a sigh of relief. And Copper suddenly came to like Gatchin.

But the two of them didn't become really good friends until a little bit after that. For Copper, that happened on the occasion of the unforgettable Fried Tofu Incident.

One day, on their way into the classroom, a friend named Hori latched onto Copper and said in a low voice, "You know about Uragawa? I hear that now everyone is calling him Fried Tofu."

"Really?" This was news to Copper. So when he asked why this was so, Hori, who was famous for gossip, explained while a sly smile floated up onto his face.

"Because that kid Uragawa always brings fried tofu in his lunch box, every day. And it's not even cooked with anything, just plain fried tofu."

"Huh."

"I heard that since this semester started, he's had fried tofu every single day, except maybe four days. That's probably why it always smells like fried tofu around Uragawa."

Copper thought that this was kind of an unpleasant story. "Okay," he said, "but how did you learn that?"

"That is, well . . ." And here Hori, after scanning the vicinity a little, now dropped his voice to a real whisper. "It's a secret, but you know Yamaguchi, who sits next to Uragawa? Every day, he's been quietly, carefully watching him, I heard. And then he told all his friends. But look, this is still a secret, okay? You didn't hear it from me! Because Uragawa himself doesn't even know yet."

Listening to this story, Copper had an ugly feeling. It seemed that listening to these rumors and spreading the nickname was no better than what Yamaguchi was doing, sneaking and spying on a person's lunch box every day and sharing the news.

Copper had seldom eaten fried tofu. On the rare occasions that it appeared at his dinner table, he usually finished his meal without touching it. There was something about it he just couldn't stomach.

And despite that, Uragawa was eating it every day—well, in all honesty, that did make Copper curious. But at the moment, Uragawa was stuck with it as a nickname, without knowing anything about it at all, which was somehow pitiful, and Copper didn't have the heart to snicker about it together with Hori.

Even leaving that aside, everyone had teased Uragawa over all sorts of things and made fun of him all year long.

To tell the truth, one look at Uragawa was probably all anyone would need to feel that a whole lot of teasing might not be out of the question. He was of average height, but he had a disturbingly long torso. His clothes were baggy, and they didn't fit his body at all. And to top it all off, he wore a ridiculous tiny cap perched perfectly straight on his head like a soldier. Something was considerably off when it came to his physical coordination, and whether he was throwing a ball or running, he was a total mess when it came to athletic activity. Watching his uncoordinated movement, you couldn't help but think of a cartoon character.

During physical education, even the teachers would sometimes burst out into unintended laughter. In gymnastics, no matter how he clung to the high bar, he couldn't manage to hoist himself up or even get a single leg over. With a heave, he would lift his rear end partway, but unable to maintain the effort, he would come flopping down, dangle there, and again lift and again fall.

Watching Uragawa flounder as he hung from the high bar, anyone might be excused for cracking a smile over the pitiful scene. In the end the teacher always had to give

Uragawa's backside a push, huffing and puffing, to help him up over the bar.

If only Uragawa had been able to hold his own when it came to schoolwork, he might have escaped being teased so often, but sadly, he wasn't particularly good at that either. Furthermore, he had a remarkable ability to fall asleep in class.

There was just one thing: no one could keep up with Uragawa at classical literature, no matter how hard they studied. In this one subject alone, his grades were amazing, far and away the best, and he could read the most difficult unannotated work calmly and easily. But to be good at the classics and to enjoy them! Regrettably, from his class-mates' point of view, it seemed like just another joke for someone who couldn't even do English and math and such to make a specialty of the classics.

His classmates, nearly all of them, teased Uragawa. Troublemakers never tired of playing tricks on him and had fun watching his flustered face.

"Uragawa, there's something on your shirt!" they might say, and when he lowered his chin to look down at his chest, they would dump a handful of gravel down the back of his collar.

If Uragawa got up from his seat for a minute dur-ing penmanship class, he'd return to find that his writing brush had disappeared. While he was under his desk, searching this way and that like a fool, the teacher would come by.

"Uragawa, what are you up to now?" The warning would come flying at him. Caught unawares as he was, Uragawa would struggle to reply.

"The brush . . ."

"What about the brush?"

"I can't find my brush."

"So you say, but weren't you just now using it? Look around carefully."

And once Uragawa was back under the desk, hopelessly looking for a brush that was nowhere to be found, just then, from a neighboring seat or the seat in front, a stealthy hand would reach out and restore the brush to its former location. Uragawa would lift his head and spot the brush, and by the time he realized that someone had hidden it, the neighboring students would all be in a state of single-minded concentration, busy with their own brushwork. There was no guessing who'd done it.

"How about it? Have you found it?" the teacher might ask.

And Uragawa might reply, "Yes, it was on my desk."

"What? That kind of carelessness will land you in trouble, you know."

In the end, every time, Uragawa just suffers the scolding on his own.

Everyone teased Uragawa this way because of his funny looks and because he was not really up to par in his schoolwork, but besides that, there was another reason.

The reason was that Uragawa's looks and belongings—really, even the way he laughed and spoke, everything about him—had the air of a country bumpkin and the smell of poverty.

Uragawa's family sold tofu and lived above their shop. His classmates, on the other hand, were the children of well-known businessmen, officials, college professors, doctors, lawyers, and so forth. Among such a group, Uragawa's upbringing never seemed to measure up, no matter what he did. There wasn't another student like Uragawa at the school, one whose collars were hand-washed at home instead of being sent out to the laundry, whose handkerchiefs were used hand towels cut in half.

If talk turned to baseball games at Jingu Stadium, Uragawa knew only the bleachers and couldn't talk about the good seats by the infield. When it came to motion pictures, Uragawa knew only the old movie hall on the outskirts of town, while his classmates went to first-class cinemas in the city center. If talk turned to a fine shopping district like the Ginza, Uragawa might go there—maybe—once every two years at best and knew nearly nothing about it, and when the others spoke of their summer resorts and ski lodges and hot springs, he had not a word to say. There was really nothing he could do to keep from being left out of everything in the worst way.

Uragawa must have felt lonely, being teased and excluded by everyone, and it must have bothered him. But he also knew that the more lonely and bothered and angry he acted, the harder the teasers would tease. So all he could do was try to respond as little as possible.

No matter what anyone did to him, he would soldier on, masking his miserable feelings with a good-natured, lonely smile.

Everyone began to think that Uragawa would never get angry no matter what they did to him. And little by little, the teasing became a regular thing. Even so, he tried not to let his feelings show. But when he was really suffering, of course, he didn't smile. Instead, he would look straight at his tormentor, with eyes that seemed as though tears might well up at any moment, and then, with an air of resignation, simply walk away.

But if Uragawa's eyes were sad at those times, there was not a hint of hatred in them. As he gazed steadily at the other person, his eyes seemed to speak.

I bear you no ill will! they seemed to say. *I would never want to bother you! So why do you cause me this endless pain? For pity's sake, let me have a moment's peace by myself!*

There was no hatred burning in those eyes, but when a decent person was caught in this gaze, it wasn't a good feeling. Because it drew out an involuntary remorse for one's own misdeeds.

So although even the good kids in the class joined in and tried teasing Uragawa once or twice, they quickly gave it up.

But Yamaguchi and his pals clung to Uragawa to the end and persisted in their cruel games.

And then something happened. This, too, was in the autumn of last year.

In November, the time came to draft a program for the class assembly. The plan was to start with an opening address, then continue with speeches, readings, and music, and conclude with entertainment, refreshments, and finally, dismissal. Professor Ogawa, who was in charge of the first-year students, ended class early so students could vote on who would perform each role.

Ballots were distributed for voting, and the professor turned to Kawase, the class monitor, and asked him to collect them once everyone had finished writing down their choices. Then, saying he had a small matter to attend to, the professor left the room. Before that, he warned everyone that it was still the middle of the period, and they must all be very quiet, since other classes were still receiving instruction.

Everyone turned immediately to their paper ballots and started thinking about whom they would choose. Copper, too, as he held his pencil, thought about it for some time. While he was doing that, a "telegram" made the rounds. When someone had something they wanted to communicate quietly during class, they would write it on a small piece of paper, and the students would pass it along under the desks, one by one, and this was called a telegram. Because the professor was not in the room at this time, the note was passed to Copper openly. On the paper, the following was written:

let's make Fried Tofu do the speech

He didn't know who the sender was, but he had no doubt it was one of Yamaguchi's crowd. It was clearly a plot to get Uragawa to stand up onstage so they could hoot and holler at him and laugh at his confusion and discomfort.

Copper barely glanced at the telegram and then passed it on. He himself wanted nothing to do with the plan written there.

The little paper made the rounds, from desk to desk in turn. With his paper ballot in front of him, Copper was still perplexed about whom to choose, but suddenly, he remembered that the telegram was making its way around to its very subject. Upon reading the telegram, Uragawa, not knowing to whom the nickname Fried Tofu belonged, was sure to be baffled.

I get it. Copper realized what was going on. *To confuse him was part of Yamaguchi's plan.*

At that point, he looked up, following the path of the telegram with his eyes. Already, the little paper had made its way to within two or three desks of Uragawa. And then, while Copper watched, it was passed into Uragawa's hand. Copper's seat was toward the back of the classroom, so he couldn't see what sort of face Uragawa made when he received the telegram, but Uragawa tilted his head to one side, as if in confusion, and sure enough, it seemed that he didn't understand its meaning. Yamaguchi, who sat next to Uragawa, twisted back and, looking toward his friends, made sure they saw him stick out his tongue and screw up his face into a grimace.

Uragawa, unknowing, passed the telegram to the seat behind him. Yamaguchi stuck his tongue out again.

The telegram continued to work its way around the room and eventually came to Yamaguchi's place. After making a show of being utterly surprised, in a voice loud enough for everyone to hear, he read out the telegram:

"'Let's make Fried Tofu do the speech,' it says . . . but who is this Fried Tofu?"

Snickers came from here and there in the classroom. Yamaguchi was in his element.

"I wonder who it's about?" And at that, he swung round toward Uragawa, asking, "Hey, Uragawa—you don't know, do you?"

Uragawa was clearly dismayed. He turned a bewildered face to Yamaguchi and shook his head in apparent embarrassment.

"I don't know."

Yamaguchi's friends burst out laughing. Others joined in, adding their voices to the laughter. When he heard that, Uragawa must have understood everything, and at that moment his face suddenly flushed.

His family business, his own lunch. That was it—Fried Tofu was him!

In a flash, he turned bright red. Even from where Copper sat, he could see the red rising all the way up to Uragawa's ears.

At that very moment, Kitami jumped up from his desk like a shot.

"Yamaguchi! You coward!" Kitami shouted, beside himself with fury. "Don't be such a bully!"

With a sidelong glance at Kitami, Yamaguchi stuck out his lower jaw and snickered defiantly. Kitami, looking as if he had lost all patience, left his seat and made straight for Yamaguchi.

"It was you who started Fried Tofu, wasn't it? You know that you did!"

"Huh? I don't know anything of the sort!"

"Then why were you sticking your tongue out before?"

"None of your business!"

Before the words had left his mouth, Kitami's palm flew straight to Yamaguchi's cheek with a smack. Yamaguchi turned pale. He glared at Kitami, eyes full of hate, and then, out of the blue, suddenly spat at him. It was a direct hit on Kitami's face.

"Let's go!" shouted Kitami, heaving the full weight of his bulldog body right at Yamaguchi. There was the sound of chairs tipping, the two bodies tangled, and they tumbled down between the desks. Yamaguchi landed faceup, pinned beneath Kitami.

Yamaguchi was much taller than Kitami but was no match for him when it came to sheer strength. He tried to push him off, struggling, but was unable to break free, and while the other students watched, he was pummeled repeatedly in the head. Kitami grabbed Yamaguchi by the lapels of his jacket and shook him up and down. His head hit the floor with an audible noise.

Up to this point Copper had been able to see by craning his neck, but now the entire class rose as one, and everyone rushed toward the two boys. Copper, too, jumped up and pushed forward, but by then a throng of people had formed a circle around them, and he couldn't tell what was going on inside it. When he pushed through the crowd and neared his two classmates, he came upon a truly unexpected scene.

As before, Yamaguchi was pinned on his back in the narrow space between the two desks. Kitami was still holding him down from above, glaring at him hatefully.

But now, behind Kitami, clinging to his back, there was Uragawa.

"I'm okay, Kitami! Don't do it! I'm okay!"

While saying this, Uragawa was trying with all his might to restrain Kitami, who was still on the attack. Uragawa's voice sounded like he was about to burst into tears.

"It doesn't matter! Please—just let him go!"

Kawase, the class monitor, was also earnestly trying to calm Kitami. Silent and out of breath, Kitami continued to glare at Yamaguchi.

But then the professor's voice rang out.

"Just what is going on here?"

A dead silence fell over the classroom, the students glancing sidelong at each other.

"Everyone, return to your seats!"

As the students filed back to their seats, Kitami and Yamaguchi released each other and stood up. On inspection, Kitami's hand was bleeding. While Yamaguchi had been pinned, he had dug his fingernails into Kitami's hand as hard as he could. Kitami had returned to his seat, so Yamaguchi took a seat as well, still fuming.

Once the group was seated, Professor Ogawa let loose.

"What in the world have you been up to here? After what I said earlier, you start this kind of fuss the moment I'm out of the room! And you expect to become first-rate students? If you were at all mindful of the work going on in other rooms, you'd refrain from this kind of commotion, no matter what the circumstances are. It's a terrible shame."

The professor went on, looking at both Yamaguchi and Kitami in turn.

"It's not often that people need to settle an argument with violence. What in the world were you arguing about?"

The two boys said not a word.

"Very well. We'll talk about that later. Now then, between the two of you, who first lifted a hand against the other? Tell me that."

"I did," Kitami answered plainly.

"Is that right? You had to speak with your fists? You didn't know how to say it with your mouth—is that it?"

"I didn't think so."

"What in the world caused you to act so rashly? It can't have been for no reason at all."

"..."

"Try to say something, if you can. Why would you act with such violence?"

Still, Kitami remained silent.

"Please be honest. In starting a fight and creating this commotion, you are thoroughly in the wrong. But you are still young. Your character is still in formation. If you were unable to restrain your anger, you needn't necessarily be condemned for that. If one were to feel that this act was not entirely without cause or reason, one might in that case expect to see more restraint from you in the future. Now is the time to speak."

Even spoken to in that way, Kitami, face downcast, made no word of reply.

Copper didn't understand why Kitami was keeping silent. If he would just state the plain truth of the matter, then the professor would learn about the rotten behavior of Yamaguchi and his friends, and Kitami would get off without being scolded so badly.

"You can't say it, eh? I see. Well then, Kawase, let's hear it from you. Tell us exactly what you saw."

As the professor said this, the bell signaling the end of class rang out. At that, the professor told Yamaguchi, Kitami, and Kawase to remain behind, all three of them, while he dismissed the remaining students to the playground.

✳

Even after leaving for the playground, Copper couldn't help but worry about the professor's investigation. So during recess he remained under the parasol tree by the school doors, talking with Mizutani and waiting for the three students to emerge.

The three of them came out just before the next period was to start. First to emerge was Kawase, with a terribly serious look on his face. Everyone gathered around him to ask about the professor's verdict. The next to come out was Yamaguchi. Yamaguchi's buddies ran over to him, and they muttered together, but presently they surrounded him and bore him off somewhere, still sulking.

The last one out was Kitami. He was whistling as he exited and had a bright expression on his face. Watching him, Copper was relieved. It seemed certain that he had not been scolded much at all.

Uragawa ran to Kitami, faster than anyone else. Then he asked him something anxiously but must have heard some good news in response, because he lifted his head and looked happily around at everyone. Until now, Copper had never seen Uragawa with such a bright expression on his face.

By Kawase's telling, it seemed that once all the explanations had been made and the professor understood all the circumstances, Yamaguchi received a severe scolding. Kitami also received a warning, but he wasn't scolded so heavily.

On his way home on the day all this happened, Copper was with Kitami. He asked Kitami why he hadn't explained himself when the professor questioned him. Kitami replied, "Wouldn't that make me a rat? I hate that." He stroked his face with his bandaged hand. When they had come as far as the train station and it was time to part ways, Copper turned to Kitami and said, "This Sunday, do you want to come play at my house? Mizutani is coming, too."

On True Experience

~~~~~~

Dear Copper,

Thank you for sharing the story of the Fried Tofu Incident with me yesterday. I could see you were excited, and I found the story deeply interesting as well. To hear you express your support for Kitami and your sympathy for Uragawa, well, that was no surprise, but all the same, it made me happy to hear it. Suppose for a minute that you were among those friends of Yamaguchi instead, skulking off with him to some corner of the playground after being scolded by the teacher. You can't know how unbearable that would be to your mother, and to me.

What your mother and I want more than anything is for you to grow up into a good person. Those were also your father's final wishes.

So when I see that you hate that which is low minded, crude, and prejudiced, and that you show respect for an honest, brave spirit—how shall I put it? That comes as a tremendous relief.

I haven't spoken to you about this yet, but three days before he passed away, your father called me to his side. He said that he needed to ask me a favor and it had to do with you. Then he related his hopes.

"I want him to become a great man! A fine example of a human being."

I commit these words to paper, here in this book, for you.

You must hold them close and never forget them. I bear them in mind myself and think that I will not forget them either.

When I write things in the notebook for you to read someday, it's because of those words that your father said to me.

At times in your life, you have already come to think in earnest about the world and people's lives. So I will speak to you seriously about such matters, without even half joking. Because when it comes to things like this, you can't become a great man without having great thoughts.

Even so, there's no point in telling you, "The world is like this. People's lives are like that." There's no way anyone can explain such things in a word or two to you. And even if there were, it's not the sort of thing where you could just listen and take it all in and say right away, "Okay, now I get it."

When it comes to English, geometry, algebra—even someone like me could teach you these. However, people come together and build this world, and they live their different lives in it individually, and I cannot teach you what that means or what value it all has. That is something you must discover on your own as you get older—and even after that, when you are grown, you will have to study this and seek out the answers for yourself.

You know that water comes from oxygen and hydrogen, don't you? And you're aware that in water these are in a ratio of one part to two. This sort of thing can be fully explained in words, and what's more, you can watch an experiment in class and say to yourself, "Aha! I see how it works!"

But when it comes to the taste of cold water, there's no way to teach that other than letting you drink the water yourself. No matter how anyone tries to explain, you're not going to understand the actual taste unless you have that experience.

In the same way, there's no way to explain the color red to anyone who hasn't seen it with their own living eyes. Because it's something a person starts to understand only when the color red meets their eyes in reality.

There are lots of things like this in life.

For example, a person discovers the pleasures of painting, sculpture, and music only by experiencing them. You will never be able to make someone understand this if they have not encountered great art. And for this subject in particular, we need more than our ordinary eyes and ears. To appreciate art, you must use your inner eyes and ears. You must open your heart.

And your heart, well, it opens only when you actually encounter a great work of art in person and it makes a deep impression on you. If it means anything at all to live in this world, it's that you must live your life like a true human being and feel just what you feel. This is not something that anyone can teach from the sidelines, no matter how great a person they may be.

Of course, there are many great philosophers and Buddhist monks from long ago who have left us words of wisdom about this matter. Even today, our true thinkers and scholars struggle painfully, trying to unravel the problem. And then they pour these thoughts of theirs into their work. Even if they are not preaching—as priests or monks do, for example—that sort of wisdom is still at the root of everything they write.

In the years to come, you will slowly begin to read these works and study the ideas of great people. But even when you have read the books and learned the ideas, the ultimate key to the mystery will be—Copper, of course it will be you. You, yourself and no other. For it is only through the life you will lead, building on your many experiences and impressions, that you will be able to understand the truths in the words of these great thinkers. You will never really know these writings just by reading them, the way you would study mathematics or chemistry.

That is why I think the first, most basic step in these matters is to start with the moments of real feeling in your life, when your heart is truly moved, and to think about the meaning of those. The things that you feel most deeply, from the very bottom of your heart, will never deceive you in the slightest. And so at all times, in all things, whatever feelings you may have, consider these carefully.

If you do this, then someday, somewhere, a unique, once-in-a-lifetime experience will leave a deep impression on you, and you will come to understand something that has a meaning that is not just limited to that one moment. That thought will be an idea that is truly your own.

To put it a slightly more difficult way, you must make a habit of thinking honestly, with your own experience as a foundation, and—Copper, this is very important!—if someone fakes this part, no matter what kind of great-sounding things they think or say, they are all lies in the end.

Like your father, your mother and I also want you to become a great person. We hope more than anything that you will think great thoughts about the world and what it means to be human, and also that you will actually lead a great life in accordance with those thoughts. So it's all the more important to me that you grasp well what I have said.

Although your mother and I do want you to become great with all our hearts, that doesn't mean we only want you to study, behave yourself, and be a perfect student, faultless in the eyes of your teachers and friends.

Nor am I saying that in the future you should become a perfect adult, a person free of all criticism or blame.

That is to say, of course good grades are good, and bad behavior will cause you trouble, and once you're out in the world, I want you to lead an unimpeachable life, but still, those alone are not the fundamental things. There's something much more important.

Since elementary school, you've already learned quite a few things in ethics class, haven't you? When it comes to what people must do in their lives, you know there are things that must not be neglected. For instance, a person must be honest, diligent, self-sacrificing, dutiful, civic minded, kind, economical, and so on. It would be hard to find fault with such a person, if he or she existed. Such a perfect person would be respected by many and would also be worthy of such respect.

However, what I want you to consider comes after that.

Imagine you are taught to behave that way in school, and then enter the world thinking that the way to be great is to follow those rules. Then, for that reason alone, you try to do as you are told and to live as you have been taught—Copper, is that good? If you do that, you will never become your own man.

When you're a child, that's fine. However, as you get older, that's no longer enough. The most important thing—more than what other people think, more than anything—is that you should first know for yourself, truly and deeply, where human greatness lies.

Then you may feel with all your heart that you wish to become a great man. As you judge good for good, and bad for bad, case by case—and also as you actually do the things you have judged to be good—at all times, let this feeling flow through you.

Think of your friend Kitami's words: "No matter what anyone says . . . !" You must have that kind of willpower in your heart.

Otherwise, while your mother and I hope that you will become a great man, and you may think that you want to be one as well, in the end you will simply become a great-seeming man, and true greatness may always elude you.

There are lots of people in the world who act just for appearance's sake—in order to seem great in the eyes of others. That type of person worries first about how they are reflected in other people's eyes, and they inadvertently end up neglecting their true selves, as they really are. I hope you don't become that sort of person.

And that is why you absolutely must attend to the things you feel in your own heart, the things that move you deeply. That is what is most important, now and always. Do not forget this, and think carefully about what it means.

What I wrote today may be a little confusing to you. But if I were to put it simply, it's that you should collect many experiences and, while you do, always be true to that voice in your heart.

And with that, let's try to recollect the Fried Tofu Incident.

What impressed you about that?

Why were you so affected by Kitami's protest?

Why were you so deeply moved watching Uragawa trying to stop Kitami's attack on Yamaguchi?

Now then, regarding Uragawa, it's your opinion that he is lacking in self-confidence, and I feel the same. If Uragawa were able to stick up for himself, he might get by without being treated like a fool.

However, think of how hard it would be for a person in Uragawa's position to stand up to Yamaguchi without backing down. It would be fair to call such a person a hero. Anyone who criticizes Uragawa because he's not such a hero is mistaken. Because people like Uragawa deserve generosity and sympathy from the people around them.

And all the more so because Uragawa himself asked that his tormentor Yamaguchi be forgiven! In that act, he displayed a heart that was generous, sympathetic, and kind.

Chapter Three

Newton's Apple and Powdered Milk

The appointed Sunday was a perfect autumn day, crisp and clear.

The three boys had agreed that Mizutani and Kitami would finish their lunches early and come to Copper's house at one o'clock. That morning, Copper could barely manage to sit still.

Seated across the table from his mother during lunch, Copper fidgeted endlessly, wondering at every moment if he hadn't just heard the doorbell ring. He put vegetables in his mouth and stuffed some rice in after them, but even as he was chewing the food, his eyes wandered time and again to the clock on the wall. Finally, laughing, his mother said, "Please, just settle down a bit while you're eating. How many times have you looked at the clock? It must be at least fifteen already."

"Not true!" Copper protested, reddening slightly. "It's less than ten!"

"Ten times, then, but isn't that enough? There, you did it again just now."

"That's not fair, Mom! That time I was looking at the calendar. No cheating!"

"What a thing to say. Well, never mind, just please drink your tea. You'll give yourself indigestion if you don't settle down. Don't fret—you'll see them soon enough."

They finished their meal. It was twenty minutes to one. Copper sprawled in the parlor, reading the newspaper commentary on the Tokyo Big Six baseball game. Fourteen minutes to one. He had examined the Sunday comics from start to finish. Ten minutes to one. He read a report on a visit to the zoo. Still seven more minutes to go . . .

"Aaaaargh!" Copper finally tossed the newspaper aside and let out a woeful cry.

"What can you be up to now?" His mother broke into a chuckle. "You're just having a terrible time waiting, aren't you? I wonder who's coming? How will we ever entertain them?"

The long hand of the clock slowly inched its way toward twelve. And then, with a little click, the hand advanced and the clock chimed once. It was one o'clock. Copper had just decided it might be a good idea to run down to the train station to check on them, when the sound of the doorbell rang out from the pantry.

Copper dashed to the front hall, and there stood Kitami, looking pleased to have arrived at one o'clock on the dot. About fifteen minutes later, Mizutani also showed up.

The three of them played various games in Copper's room on the second floor until around three o'clock. Cards, crokinole, chess, Sherlock Holmes—they had a great time. Copper and Mizutani always had fun when the two of them played together, but it was quiet. Today, the addition of Kitami brought new life to the party. Over and over, the three of them laughed until their sides hurt.

Once they had played all the usual indoor games, Copper spoke up: "Shall we listen to the Waseda-Keio baseball game?"

"College baseball? Do you have a recording of it?"

"No, on the radio. I'll broadcast it."

"Huh?"

Copper unplugged the radio and set it on the desk. Then he threw a large cloth over his head and squatted down.

Soon enough the broadcast began.

". . . The deep-blue sky clears, the wind falls, and the dust has settled in Meiji Jingu Stadium. The rising sun on the flag of Japan is just barely waving in the wind behind center field, and it's an absolutely perfect day for a ball game. An absolutely perfect day . . ."

"Cool!" Kitami shouted.

"Waseda University, the champions of North Tokyo! Keio University, the champions of South Tokyo!"

Copper continued in a grand voice.

"This battle between two great college teams said to be the jewels of our baseball world is now in its thirtieth year! Even now, millions of fans across the country go wild with excitement. The honor of the two schools, the hopes of alumni and students, and thirty years of tradition—just think, it all comes down to this one contest . . ."

Of course, it was pretty clever. Especially since Copper was saying it all himself.

". . . Thirty minutes before the heated battle, Jingu Stadium is buzzing with anticipation and emotion. Tens of thousands of fans have been streaming into the great stadium around the field since early this morning, and at this point there's barely room to stand. The cheering squads for each school have occupied their sections along the infield and outfield and jammed their seats to overflowing. With Keio on the third-base side and Waseda on the first-base side, each commanding their own brass band, they have been sounding off fiercely since before the match . . ."

"What about the players?" Mizutani broke in.

"I'm going to do them now," the radio replied.

"Now the Waseda players are entering from the first-base side. The Waseda players are entering. They are wearing their matching gray jerseys. The crowd is on its feet, standing as one! Just listen to that—the applause is thunderous. Waseda's cheering section is on their feet. It's the welcoming chant for the players."

At that point, in a voice as loud as he could possibly get, Copper began to sing the Waseda fight song:

> *"Deep-blue sky, the golden sun above,*
> *Shining brightly far and wide, that's our history . . ."*

Kitami quickly backed him up, and they sang:

> *"Brilliant and superior, our fighting spirit burns,*
> *To the throne of victory . . ."*

However, it's not easy for two people to take the place of an entire cheering section. So Kitami raised his voice to a fearsome bellow:

> *"Waseda! Waseda!*
> *Victory to Waseda!"*

". . . And to continue, from the third-base side, Keio enters! Led by team manager Morita, the Keio players take the field. And to greet them, the Keio cheer section begins their fight song! Listen now. It's a magnificent chorus."

This time Copper changed his style and sang in a high voice.

"Youth with blood that burns so fierce,
We are shining, oh so bright."

And then Mizutani joined in the chant with his clear voice.

"Eyes upon the star of hope—
As we march on to victory,
And our power ever new,
Look! Our finest gather now . . ."

The radio continued the broadcast.

"Both sides have begun their warm-up. The Waseda players spread out on the field. It's time for batting practice. And now let's review the history of this war of two teams, starting in the year 1905 . . ."

"That's enough of that!" Kitami said.

"But if I don't say it like that, it won't be like the Waseda-Keio game!" the radio protested in a grumbling tone.

"But that's okay. It's better if the game starts quickly."

"You think so? Fine, we can do it that way . . ." The radio seemed to think it a shame to waste its hard-won knowledge but quickly followed Kitami's orders.

"Already now both sides have completed their fielding practice, and it seems that they are just about ready to start the game. First up is Waseda. Keio is defending in the field. Keio's pitcher is Kusumoto. He takes the mound with a confident smile. Waseda's leadoff man, Satake, enters the batter's box. Play ball!"

Suddenly Copper howled in a strange voice: "OO, OO, OOWOO!" This was meant to be the starting whistle for the game.

So the game started, but as it progressed, it eventually descended into chaos. At first, both sides had scoreless turns, but after Waseda scored a run during the fourth inning, each team had hits every inning, and every inning, there were runs scored. At any rate, whenever Keio scored, no matter whether it was one run or two, Kitami would say, "Hey! No way!"

So then Copper would give Waseda one or two runs, taking advantage of errors by Keio. But when he did that, Mizutani would lodge a protest: "Don't have Keio make so many errors!"

Copper the Commentator took great pains to advance the game in such a way as to suit both of his friends. He had no choice but to make it a furious seesaw of a game. The closely fought back-and-forth battle continued, and at long last they came to the bottom of the ninth inning. Waseda was in the field, Keio at bat, and Waseda had the lead by one run.

"Runners on first and third! Keio's batter is the team captain, Kachikawa. The fielders are on high alert, and number three, the great Kachikawa, has a heavy burden on his shoulders. There are already two outs, but with a runner on third, there's the chance for a hit-and-run! With a single hit here, just like that, the game will be tied. The count is three and one. Perhaps the veteran pitcher Wakahara will throw a fourth ball for the intentional walk, in hopes of taking out the next batter."

"No way! Make it a strikeout!" Kitami shouted.

"Wakahara addresses the plate. He goes into his stretch and puts the fifth ball in motion. The pitch. The swing. He makes contact! The ball rises, up, up, up, heading toward deep left field. The left fielder is backing up hard. Back . . . Back . . . Oh, it's way past him! The ball flies over the left fielder's head and lands beneath the grandstand bleachers. The lead runner scores! The other runner takes off from first like a rabbit.

"He's rounding third base and heading for home. Oh, and he crosses the plate. Another score! Keio wins, Keio wins, Keio wins! Kachikawa hits a towering triple, Keio scores two runs, and just like that, the game is over. OO, OO, OOWOO!"

But the whistle couldn't end the game. Because Kitami had jumped up and hurled himself at Copper the Radio.

"Hey! Radio! Can't you shut up?"

As he said this, Kitami yanked down on the cloth that was covering Copper's head.

"Ow! That's rough! Help!" Copper yelled from inside the cloth. "And just now, a hooligan has appeared on the field."

"Hey! Will you shut up, I said! Stop talking!"

"The hoo . . . the hoo . . . the hooligan is a Waseda supporter!"

"HEY!!!"

Kitami, whose face had turned bright red with laughter, pushed down with all his might on Copper. Under attack, Copper continued all the same.

"The hooligan . . . has inter . . . interrupted the broadcast. The commentator is now in a life-or-death struggle!"

Kitami burst out laughing. Copper seized the moment to try to stand up, and the two of them toppled, tangled together, beside the desk. The radio was jostled and started to tumble off the desk, but Mizutani launched himself at it and tackled it.

Kitami let go, and Copper took the cloth off his head. The two of them sprawled on the tatami mat, still laughing.

Copper's head was on Kitami's stomach, and every time Kitami laughed, the vibrations from his stomach shook Copper's head with a little jolt.

"Ah, I'm beat." Copper flopped on the floor in an exhausted pose. Kitami, too, stretched out his arms and took a breather. At this, Mizutani heaved a deep sigh and threw himself down next to them.

The three of them lay there quietly for a while. They already felt close enough that there was no need to speak. How nice it was just to lie there in silence.

Outside it was a perfect autumn day, crisp and clear. Framed by the trees in the garden, the roofs of the neighboring houses were just barely visible through the wide-open sliding shoji doors at the end of the hall, and over the fence was the bright-blue autumn sky. Across the sky, clouds as light as spun silk flowed slowly by, their shapes shifting as they went.

Copper lay there absentmindedly, while off in the distance a train rolled by, its sound playing dreamily in his ears.

Mizutani and Kitami went home after dark.

After the radio battle between Waseda and Keio, the three boys had gone out to the field for batting practice and then played catch until evening. They'd come back in for dinner, and the sun had set while they were eating. Then

Copper's uncle had dropped by for a visit, so for a while the conversation had turned lively, but because all three boys were still in their first year of junior high, Mizutani and Kitami couldn't stay late. When they heard the seven o'clock bell ring, the two of them had to go. Copper and his uncle went out to see them off.

It was a fine moonlit night. The moon had just risen, and its glowing face peered round the broad trunks of the keyaki trees. It was the tenth day of its cycle, bright and almost full. As they walked along the dark, hedge-lined street, the moonlight through the twin rows of trees alternately illuminated the four faces in the darkness and then winked out again. The ceramic-tiled roofs glowed as if they were wet, and the night air was already cold enough for a jacket.

When they looked up, the sky showed clearly through the tall treetops, which had already shed most of their leaves. The night sky spreading above was indigo blue, deep enough to make them shiver, and in it the stars shone small and high, as if they were holes poked through by the tip of a needle.

It's so beautiful! Copper thought. It was the sort of crisp, clear autumn evening that closed tightly around his body and made him want to breathe deeply.

The four of them walked slowly through the quiet suburban residential neighborhood toward the train station. There was still quite a way to go to reach the noisy streets in the vicinity of the station.

Mizutani turned to Copper.

"The story your uncle was telling us before, did you understand it? You know, about Newton?"

"Not really."

"It was strange, wasn't it? What was it about?"

As he spoke, Mizutani looked up at the moon. Its light shone full onto his pale face. Copper, too, lifted his head and gazed upward. The moon looked as if it had been hung there, suspended in the middle of the sky, and the two of them fell silent at the strange scene. Then Copper remembered that from the ground where they were standing to the moon was an impossibly far distance.

Over such a great distance, he thought, *all the way from the earth to the moon up there, an invisible power is working.*

An inexpressibly distant feeling came over Copper. He turned to his uncle.

"Uncle, can you explain what you were saying before about Newton?"

The Newton story was something that Copper's uncle had brought up while they were having some fruit for dessert after dinner. Peeling an apple in a single unbroken strand, the uncle had said what the boys were now trying to remember:

"You all know the story of Newton's apple, don't you? Watching an apple fall, he came up with his law of gravity. But, I wonder, how was he able to realize something like that just from watching an apple fall? Do any of you know?"

None of the three boys knew. Then his uncle asked, "Did you ever wonder why?"

The three of them of course were silent, shaking their heads.

"No?" he asked, inclining his head slightly, but just at that moment, he finished peeling the apple, and the skin dropped onto the tray. So Copper's uncle set Newton aside and instead focused on eating the apple.

"Mm, this is a good apple. Where's it from?"

The conversation turned to a comparison of Aomori apples and Hokkaido apples, and in the end neither Mizutani nor Copper had an opportunity to ask the uncle more. This was what Mizutani remembered on the road home.

Prodded by Copper, his uncle remembered the conversation.

"Yes, yes. That's right. We were just about to talk about that, weren't we?"

The uncle stopped for a moment, lit up a cigarette, and then resumed walking slowly while he started to speak.

"Around the time that I was starting elementary school, one day I saw, in a special New Year's supplement to the newspaper, a page with three large full-color prints. One of the panels was a picture of Emperor Buretsu kicking a wild boar to death, another was the mother of the philosopher Mencius—she had stopped her work at a weaving loom and was scolding her son—and the last one was a picture of Isaac Newton, standing and looking at an apple that had fallen from a tree.

"Of course, to me they were just three pictures, and I didn't understand what they meant at all. At that point, my older sister—Copper, that's your mother—she read the captions for the three panels and explained them to me, one by one.

"I believe your mother would have been in high school by that time. She must have been just a year or two older than the three of you are now. In any case, she read the captions and was kind enough to read them again with me and talk to me about each one. To me at that time, your mother seemed so great.

"By the way, to this very day, I still don't understand why the newspaper publisher had seen fit to put these three images together, but—well, let me tell you what I learned about the meanings of each of the pictures, and you'll see.

"A long time ago in Japan, there lived a brave emperor named Buretsu, and when he went on a hunt, it seems that he brought down a wild boar with a single blow. That was the first one. The second was about a Chinese wise man named Mencius, whose mother was also very wise and scolded her son when he quit school, sending him back to his studies. The third was a picture of a great scholar named Newton, who made the tremendous discovery of his law of universal gravitation while watching an apple fall—up to this point, even an elementary school student like me could follow, you see.

"The story of the brave emperor was the easiest of the three to understand. Even the story of the wise man's mother was easy to get when my sister explained it—that Mencius leaving school in the middle of his studies would be as bad as her cutting off her weaving in the middle of the loom. But take the story of Newton one step further, and what does it mean? Well, I was stumped. I had no idea.

"Listening to my sister's—well, your mother's— explanation of the Newton picture, I asked her this question: 'Why?' And when I did, then your mother was in trouble, too, you see? Because to make sense of this for a student as young as I was, first she had to explain the relationships between the earth and moon, the earth and sun, and various planetary bodies. I remember it to this day—your mother took out a rubber ball and a Ping-Pong ball and said, 'This is the planet earth, where we live. And this is the moon. When you do this, it goes like that.' Over and over, she patiently tried somehow to explain it to me.

"But when your partner is a first grader, no matter how deliberately and passionately you explain, you're fighting an uphill battle. And I even remember listening with a strange feeling, not sure if I understood or not. And finally, back then, your mother made a distressed face and said, 'Are you still confused? Well, when you get older, you'll understand.' And that was the end of the matter.

"Before, when we were eating the apple—or, more precisely, when I was peeling the apple—the memory of that time came back to me."

"But, Uncle, when did you learn the answer?" Copper asked. Deep inside, he couldn't help hoping that his uncle had finally figured it out when he was around Copper's own age.

His uncle continued.

"It's strange! During elementary school, I learned most of the basics of the solar system and the relationship between the earth and the moon and so forth, all of those things that your mother was at her wit's end trying to get me to understand. And once I was in junior high, like you, I was taught all sorts of things about such matters, and it all became everyday common sense.

"But still, even after that, I didn't understand at all how

an apple falling could, in Newton's head, evolve into the idea of his law of universal gravitation.

"Even though I had been able to learn the law of gravity, more or less, and why celestial bodies move the way they do, the question of how he came to know all that from an apple still confused me, same as before."

"So when did you figure it out?" Copper was intensely curious.

His uncle replied, "It puzzled me, but I suppose I didn't have a burning need to know. I sat on the problem for a long time, until I was a student in college!"

"What? A college student?" Copper's eyes widened. Kitami, too, let out a laugh.

"That's right. I made it all the way to college without understanding this. I muddled along all that time, thinking vaguely about it, something like this: Newton was probably deep in thought, mulling over a physics problem, when suddenly, the thump of an apple falling disturbed the peace. Surprised by this, he came to his senses with a start, and the wonderful idea must have just been sparkling there, like a flash of lightning."

"But it wasn't like that?" This time, it was Kitami who asked.

"That's right. Actually, scholars say that it's doubtful how much truth there is to this story of discovering the theory of universal gravitation from an apple, so I honestly don't know how it was in reality. But once I was a college student, at some point, I asked a friend who was enrolled as a science student, and this friend said he had an idea of how Newton might have been thinking. He explained it to me, and for the first time, I thought, *Of course, that seems right*."

"What was the explanation?" "Will we understand, too?" asked Copper and Mizutani, one after the other. The uncle took a lazy drag on his cigarette and continued speaking.

"Oh, you'll understand. 'Of course,' said my friend, 'when the apple first fell, it may have felt no different from having a flash of insight.' But what matters came after that.

"The apple probably fell from a height of, oh, let's say three or four meters, but Newton might have tried to think, *Well, what if it were ten meters instead of four? Of course*, if the four meters were ten meters, the result would be the same. The apple would fall.

"Then what if it were fifteen meters? Naturally, it's going to fall, right? And twenty meters? The same. If we gradually increase the height to a hundred meters or two hundred meters, no matter what number of meters we consider, the apple still falls, in accordance with the law of gravity.

"But let's consider what happens if we increase the height of the apple more and more, until we reach the point where it's thousands or tens of thousands of meters in the air. Eventually the apple gets to the height of the moon. In that case, would the apple fall? As long as gravity is working, certainly we expect it to fall. In fact, it's not just apples, is it? We expect that anything must fall. But what about the moon? The moon doesn't fall, does it?"

This time neither Copper nor Mizutani nor Kitami uttered a word; they just waited for his uncle to continue. At this time the four of them had emerged from the tree-lined street and were walking along the road beside open fields. Above the two-story houses facing the fields, the moon was shining down silently as ever on the four of them.

"The moon doesn't fall. This is because the force of the earth tugging on the moon and the force of the moon trying to fly off somewhere as it spins round the earth—these two forces—are perfectly balanced.

"By the way, Newton was by no means the first to come up with the idea that gravity is working between celestial bodies in this way. Even back in Kepler's era, they suspected that there was gravity between the planets and the sun and that was the reason the planets maintain a perfect orbit as they spin. Moreover, the idea that a thing will fall to the ground if there's no force to support it, this was well known even before Newton. It's known as Galileo's law of falling bodies.

"So what was Newton's big discovery? It was to show that if you link these two forces—gravity working on objects on earth, and gravitation working between celestial bodies—it becomes clear that they have the same nature. So, you see, the problem that I had was really a question of why these two forces were linked in Newton's head."

The uncle took another drag on his cigarette and, after letting the ash fall, continued to speak.

"But as I said, Newton watched his apple fall and then imagined increasing the height from which the apple fell, higher and higher, until eventually he reached the moon.

"Originally, the law of gravity was a law about objects on earth. But if you separate falling objects farther and farther from the surface of the ground and lift them as far as the moon, then the relationship between those objects and the earth is no longer an earthly one. The relationship ultimately becomes celestial. Put simply, it becomes just like the relationship between two planets.

"Well, when you think like this, Copper, doesn't it seem perfectly natural to connect in your head the ideas of gravitation between two celestial bodies in the heavens and gravity working on falling objects on earth? It occurred to Newton that these two things were things of the same nature. And he thought, *I wonder if I could prove that?* So he started to research the subject.

"And then he calculated the distance between the earth and moon, as well as the gravity working on the moon, and the earth's force of gravitation, and so on, and after a long time and much hard work, eventually he was able to prove his idea. And as a result, using a single physical principle, he was able to explain very neatly both the motion linking the web of stars spinning round and round through the enormous universe and the motion of a single dewdrop falling from the grass.

"In other words, you see, with a single law of physics, he was able to explain both the things of heaven and the things of earth. From the point of view of academic history, this was, of course, an exceptionally great undertaking . . ."

Finishing his story, Copper's uncle tossed away the cigarette he was smoking. The red flame described a parabola as it fell to the ground and winked out.

"How about it, Copper? Do you understand?"

Instead of replying, Copper silently nodded his head. Kitami and Mizutani were completely silent as well. The three of them were all uncertain as to how to put their feelings into words. So his uncle started talking again.

"What made Newton great was not just that he wondered whether gravity and gravitation might be one and the same. It's that he took great pains and made such an effort to confirm his idea. This was a complicated problem that would have been so confusing as to be nearly impossible for an ordinary person, you see?

"But again, if he had never had that first idea, he never

would have started all that research, so the idea is also quite important.

"Incidentally, when my friend gave me the explanation I just related to you, I thought it over thoroughly, and this kind of great idea comes from a surprisingly simple place. Or so I believe. In Newton's case it comes from taking an apple that has fallen from a height of three or four meters and lifting it, in his head, higher and higher, until he comes to a certain place and, with a thud, collides with a bigger idea.

"So you see, Copper, the things that we call obvious are tricky. When you think about a thing as if it were self-evident and follow it wherever it may lead, soon enough you run into a thing that you can no longer call self-evident. This is not only true when it comes to the science of physics . . ."

The moon was already a great deal higher. It gazed diagonally down at the four figures from above, silent as always. Above their heads spread the vast, limitless night sky, and the stars twinkled ceaselessly. On a night like this, to think about the distant celestial world was to feel that one was disappearing into the atmosphere.

Copper and his companions were suffused with pale light. The gravel covering the road along which the four of them were walking was drenched in moonlight and shone with a lovely glow.

A little while later, Copper and his uncle hurried home along the same road. They were returning from seeing Mizutani and Kitami to the train station. The chill of the night air had seeped into their bones. They hardly spoke a word. In the sky, the moon, without anger, laughter, or tears, with a quiet countenance over the rooftops and telephone poles, slipped past the boughs of the keyaki trees and followed the two of them as they walked.

When they came to the front of Copper's house, his uncle slowed to a halt.

"Well, see you soon . . ." he said. The two of them said their goodbyes.

"Good night, Uncle."

"Yes, good night to you as well."

On a Friday, the fifth day after these events, something unusual happened. A long letter from Copper arrived at his uncle's place.

Dear Uncle,

The last time I saw you, I wanted to tell you something, but then I thought it would be better to write it in a letter, so I did.

I made a discovery. It definitely came from listening to your story of Newton. But if I told everyone that I made a discovery, they would laugh at me. So I am only telling you. Please don't say anything about it for now, even to my mother.

I call the discovery the Net Rule of Human Particle Relations. At first I was thinking of calling it the Powdered-Milk Secret, but it sounded too much like a detective story in one of my magazines, so I gave that up. If you could think of a better name, I would like that.

I am still having trouble explaining my discovery, but if I tell you step by step how I made it, I think you will probably understand.

It started when powdered milk came into my head. That's the reason I think everybody would probably laugh at me if I talked about it. I wanted to think of something greater than that, but powdered milk came up on its own, so there was nothing I could do about that.

On Monday, I woke up in the middle of the night. I was dreaming something and woke up, but I forget what the dream was. When I woke up, for some reason, I was thinking of powdered-milk canisters. At our house we have those big ones that say "Lactogen" on them that we put biscuits or rice crackers in.

So then I remembered what mother said. One time she

told me that when I was a baby, she didn't have enough milk for me, so I grew up drinking Lactogen every day. She said that now the Lactogen cans remind her of those days.

When I heard that, I said, well, then cows in Australia are also my mothers, aren't they? Because Lactogen comes from Australia, and there's even a map of Australia on the can. While I was lying in bed, I remembered that. Then I imagined lots of things about Australia. I thought of ranches and cows and Aboriginal peoples and powdered-milk factories and ports and steamships and more, one thing after another.

And that's when I remembered your Newton story. You told us how Newton had arrived at a fantastic idea by taking an apple that fell from three or four meters, right? And imagining it higher and higher, and thinking about it all the way.

So I wondered, What would happen if I thought about the things that were connected with powdered milk, as far as I could think?

Lying in bed, I tried to think how powdered milk would get from Australia's cows to my mouth, every step of the way. When I did that, it went on forever, and I was really amazed. Because there were so many people that appeared. I will try to write them all down.

1. Before the Milk Comes to Japan

The cows, the people who take care of the cows, the people who milk the cows, the people who take the milk to the factory, the people who make it into powder at the factory, the people who put it in canisters, the people who pack up all the canisters, the people who take them by truck or however to the railway, the people who load them on the steam trains, the people who run the trains, the people who take the cans from the trains to the harbor, the people who load them on the steamship, the people who run the steamship.

2. After the Milk Comes to Japan

The people who unload the steamship cargo, the people who take the cargo to the steam train, the people who take it to the warehouse, the warehouse guards, the merchants who sell it, the people who advertise it, the pharmacy that buys it, the person who takes it to the pharmacy, the pharmacist, the delivery boy who brings the milk to the kitchen of our house. (Tomorrow night I'll write what happens after that.)

(Continued from last night)

I realized that to get from Australia to me when I was a baby, the powdered milk had to run a very, very long relay race. And I thought that if you added in all the thousands or tens of thousands of people who built the factories and steam trains and steamships, then there were lots and lots of people who were all connected to me.

But among all those people, the only one I really knew was the pharmacist near our old house, and other than him, I didn't know any of them. And looking at it the other way around, I was sure none of them knew me. I thought that was really strange.

And then I thought about the darkened lamp, the clock, the desk, the tatami mats, and all the other things I could see from the bed, one after another. When I did, whichever I thought of, they were all the same as the Lactogen. Behind them were so many people that I couldn't count them, all connected, each one to the next. But they were all people I had never seen and didn't know, and I really didn't know what their faces were like.

That night I had a lot more thoughts, but I was getting tired and I fell asleep, so I forgot them. But the next day I only remembered what I just told you.

I think this is a discovery. Because even though I never thought about it at all until now, when I do think about it, I can understand that everything and everyone, everywhere, is like that.

On the way to school, and even after I went to school, I tried to think about everything I saw, no matter how random, but no matter what it was, they were all the same. And I could tell that all those countless people weren't just connected to me.

In my classroom I thought carefully in detail about my teacher's wool clothes and his shoes, and I discovered that they were definitely the same. My teacher's clothes started with Australian sheep!

That's why, because of my idea, I feel that human particles are all connected like strings in a net, with countless other people that they haven't met or even seen, and without even knowing it. That's why I decided to call this the Net Rule of Human Particle Relations.

I am now applying this discovery to many things and verifying that it is not wrong in practice. Today I realized that the asphalt road is definitely like that. Also, in math class, I figured out that my teacher's head and beard were connected to the barber, and because it took a while to figure out, I got a warning from the teacher.

Still, for the sake of discovery, I think sometimes you have to live with being scolded by the teacher.

I want to write more, but mother says I have to go to sleep already. So I will end my report here. Uncle, you are the first person to know about my discovery.

On Human Relationships and the Nature of Real Discoveries

~~~~~~

Copper,

Thank you for revealing your discovery to me before any-one else in the world. I'd like to answer immediately, but since I'll be at your house tomorrow, let's meet and speak at that time.

Before we do that, I will write down a few thoughts about that letter of yours in this notebook for later. I hope someday that you will read it and remember this discovery you have made and think over my words.

I am not exaggerating when I tell you that I was truly impressed when I read your letter. To have thought all that up on your own is truly a great thing. When I was your age, I had no such thoughts. I began to think clearly about things like your discovery only after I had entered high school, and even then, it was just because I was taught them, and read them in books.

But after reading your letter, I would like you to consider a few things. I will respectfully mention one or two of these to you, Professor Copper.

You wrote in your letter that you would like me to tell you if there's a better name for your discovery than the Net Rule of Human Particle Relations. I know of one good name. It's not a name that I thought up, but rather a name that's being used now in the fields of economics and sociology.

Actually, Copper, the "human particle relations" that you have discovered are a thing that scholars call the "relations of production."

There are many things that people need to live. To do so, they take various materials from the natural world and make what they need. Some things they can take from the world to wear or eat just as they are, but even so, people end up having to do all sorts of work, such as hunting, fishing, excavating mountains, and so on. From primitive times, people have always worked. Along the way, they learned how to cooperate and to divide the work between themselves into specialties, because they had no other choice.

It is this kind of cooperation and division of work between people that scholars call "relations of production."

At first, people lived in very small clusters, scattered here and there on the earth, so this kind of cooperation and division of labor was practiced only within narrow areas. At that time, people could see clearly whose hard work had supplied the things that they ate and wore.

In all likelihood, everyone knew each other by sight, and the goods they produced were all very simple things, and no doubt people all worked together, at first, at hunting and fishing. So they probably knew without thinking whom to thank for the things they ate and wore.

But meanwhile, those small groups of people started to trade with each other and form alliances, and gradually a communal way of living began to spread among people. The groups grew larger and eventually became what we now call countries. By this time, cooperation and specialization had already shifted to a broader scale, and relationships had become more complicated. When you looked at the things you ate or wore, there was no way to know who had worked to produce what.

The makers, too, for their part, had no idea who was eating or wearing the things that they made. They simply worked to produce different things and in return were given things that they or their families needed, or else they were given money to buy those things. And since that was the only goal, the people who were eating or wearing the things they made were of no concern to them.

And then as the ages rolled by, commerce flourished, countries even started to trade with one another, and relationships between people became more and more complex.

For instance, a Chinese farmer thinking to earn some money would raise silkworms, harvest the raw silk, and sell it, and after many twists and turns it would become a robe for a Roman nobleman.

In this way many people cooperated, not only on the production of goods but also on their transportation. They found ways to divide the work, and the many places of the world were gradually tied together, so that now the whole wide world has at last been bound up into a single network.

These days, when a Japanese silk company harvests raw silk, or a cotton company makes cloth, it's not because they think that the Japanese people need more silk or cotton. They're not even thinking that they will try to satisfy the Japanese demand first and then, if there happens to be enough left over, they will sell it in other countries. From the start, they produce these goods on a large scale, with the goal of breaking into foreign markets.

In other words, you could say that their work rests on a foundation of global connections between human beings. Japanese cotton and many other goods are needed by billions of people in India and China, and here in Japan we would currently be in a good deal of trouble without Australian wool or American petroleum.

Thus, people have been working all this time just to get what we need to live, and somewhere along the line we all became tied together as tightly as if we were segments of a great net. And just as you discovered, it's come to the point where people who have never seen or met each other have become connected in unbreakable ways. Not a soul can escape these relationships.

Of course, there are lots of people in the world who don't produce anything but are nonetheless caught in the mesh of this net. To live our lives, even for a day, we can't get by without eating and wearing clothes, so the net pulls us in. People who can eat without working have, in their own way, a very special relationship to this net.

There's more to be said about how profound relationships between the inhabitants of distantly separated countries of the world have become today, but in any case, scholars call these relationships "relations of production." In other words, by thinking of powdered milk, you have discovered these relationships.

When you are older, two fields that you will most likely have to study are economics and sociology. Scholars in these fields begin by describing how people form relationships like these in their lives, and then pursue many studies from there.

For instance, they study how these relationships have changed from one time period to another, what kind of customs and conventions have grown up on top of them, and by what rules they operate today.

Thus, your discovery became the starting point for scholars in these fields, and it is something that has been known for a long time.

You may be disappointed to hear this. You may think it's a bore that your special discovery has been known by people for a long time.

But, Copper, never let yourself feel that way. What you discovered, without anyone teaching it to you, is a great thing! Although even if it had been an academically obvious matter, I would, of course, still have respected it. To think things through to such an extent at your age is not something easily done.

But what I must ask you to put your mind to is this: What sort of discovery would be truly useful to humanity and worthy of respect from all?

It would have to be a thing that's new not just to you but to the entire human race.

People are each limited to what a single individual can experience on their own. But people have language. We can transmit our experience to others, and we can listen to the experience of others and share in that knowledge. On top of that, since we invented the alphabet, we can share our experiences with each other in writing.

Because of that, we can compare the experiences of many people in different circumstances and bring them together from all over into one place. When we unite those different points of view into the broadest possible thing, without creating contradictions, we call that a field of study.

Thus, the various fields of study may be considered to be bundles of the human experience up to now. Experiences are handed down to us from prior times, and we in turn pile our new experiences on top of these, and in this way the human race has been able to advance from a primitive state to our present state.

If people were to start again from when we were like monkeys, but this time each person on their own, we would probably remain like monkeys forever and would never attain the civilization we have now.

So we must pursue our studies as far as we are able and learn from the experiences of the people who came before us. Otherwise, all their labor will have been in vain. And since they worked so hard, it would be a mistake not to apply our efforts to problems that they didn't manage to solve. It's only through that work, which builds on all that came before, that a discovery can be considered to belong to the human race. And what's more, it's only those discoveries that we can call great.

For this reason alone, I think you will understand the need to study without any preaching from me. If you want to make great discoveries, you must now study fiercely, first and fore-most, and ascend to the summit of today's scholarship. Then work from that pinnacle.

But, Copper, remember this well. To work from up there—no, even to be able to make the climb—you must not lose the spirit that woke you in the middle of the night, to follow your own questions wherever they lead!

One last thought.

When you investigated all the things that you needed in your life, you understood that behind each one, there was a multitude of people working, in numbers greater than you could know. At the same time, those people were, from your perspective, completely unseen and unknown. You felt that this was strange, didn't you?

Because we are speaking of the whole wide world, of course it's not possible to get to know each and every one of these people. But imagine all these people who actually do the hard work to produce all those things you need—the things you eat, the things you wear, the house in which you live. They are strangers to you. And you, who are living thanks to their efforts, are a complete stranger to them. And exactly as you felt, that is certainly a strange thing.

It is strange for sure, and unfortunate, but in today's world, it's also a fact. You can honestly say that people have created a net that completely encircles the world and all of humanity, but you can't say that those connections have led to relationships that are very human at all. While the human race has progressed, conflict between human beings has continued.

In the courts, not a day goes by without a lawsuit being filed over money, and when two countries disagree, the conflict may intensify to the point of war. The "human particle relations" that you discovered are, word for word, more like the relations of physical particles and still haven't become a very "human" sort of human relations.

But needless to say, Copper, human beings must be human. For people to be in an inhuman relationship is quite a shame. Even between perfect strangers, human relationships have to be human.

Of course, having said all this, I'm not saying you have to immediately start thinking you must do this or that. I am simply saying that I hope you will think carefully about this as you grow older. Because despite all the progress of the human race up to the present, this is a problem that it has not yet been able to solve.

Now, regarding relationships that are truly human: What kind of relationships are they?

Your mother would do anything for you, without any desire for reward or compensation. To devote herself to you is, itself, her pride and joy. And as for you, isn't just doing something nice for your close friends already enough to make you happy?

There is nothing more beautiful than people nurturing goodwill toward their fellow beings. And those are the human relations that humans truly deserve. Copper, don't you agree?

~~~~~~

Chapter Four

A Friend in Need

In the schoolyard a cold wind began to blow, and the baseball season came to a close. Everyone turned to soccer with enthusiasm. Winter was steadily coming on.

December commenced with four or five days of warm weather, in which the students leaned against the south-facing school building and basked drowsily in the sun, but around the tenth of the month, suddenly a cold day came along. Then the clouds piled up, layer upon layer in the sky like old cotton, and soon the cold became bone chilling. It started to seem like snow couldn't be far away now.

In the classroom the teacher began to light the stove. When they came from the cold schoolyard into the classroom, the warm air brought a flush to their faces. And when their bodies soaked up the warmth, how sleepy they felt! Suddenly Uragawa was no longer the only one nodding off in class. Of course, he was dozing, too, frequently enough to draw some attention. Copper couldn't help but notice as Uragawa's head would slowly begin to droop and then jerk up again with a start as he caught himself napping.

Then for some reason, Uragawa was absent for two or three days. The space normally occupied by his rounded back sat empty. Copper was strangely concerned. After four or five days, there was still no sight of him.

Maybe he caught a cold, Copper guessed. When someone in the same class was absent for as many as three days, usually a good friend of the person would visit and bring word from them, but Uragawa had no close friends to do so. When he realized that, Copper suddenly wanted to go and visit him.

Saturday afternoon after school, Kitami hurried over to Copper to ask if he wanted to go play soccer.

"Hey, today let's beat those guys from the second squad! Because last time we really shouldn't have lost."

Kitami was full of spirit, but because Copper was thinking of stopping by Uragawa's house, he didn't reply with his usual "Sure, let's go!"

"I . . . Today there's something I have to do," he said.

Kitami was disappointed but finally replied, "Okay, I guess. But it's going to be boring without you." When he heard that, Copper wavered a little, but in the end he decided to go to Uragawa's place as he had originally intended, and with some resolve, he parted ways with Kitami and left through the school gates by himself.

The sky was crystal clear, and although the sun was shining, it was a cold afternoon, and the wind came in sharp, whistling gusts.

Copper exited the train at Koishikawa, in front of a large temple. A new boulevard ran up a slope to the right, leading to a large open cemetery. From the bottom of the slope, a squalid narrow street ran off to the left, barely wide enough for a car to enter, and on the right side of that street was Uragawa's house. Copper had come to this neighborhood many times to visit his father's grave, which was in the cemetery atop the slope, but it was his first time setting foot in this narrow street.

Fishmongers, greengrocers, grilled sweet potato stalls, rice merchants, candy shops—tiny stores with facades no more than three or four meters wide lined both sides of the narrow street, jostling shoulder to shoulder for room. The small, dimly lit shops had narrow eaves over their entrances, so low that any adult could reach up and touch them. Each of these shops had a second story for living quarters, and because these two-story row houses continued all the way down the street, the passage between them was somewhat dark and gloomy. Copper got the feeling that he was entering a sort of a tunnel.

For such a narrow street, the foot traffic was surprisingly busy. Women in aprons, mothers with children bound up on their backs, and many others were walking in great numbers, while youngsters in rubber boots wove in and out, ducking between them on bicycles. Children in grubby clothing darted here and there, playing samurai sword games. Strange smells wafted by on billows of air.

Copper carefully watched the right-hand side of the street as he walked. In the butcher's storefront, a heavyset man in a stained apron was busy frying something. On a half sheet of rice paper hanging down from above was written "Cutlets—10 sen, Croquettes—7 sen." At the store next door they were making *taiyaki*—fish-shaped pancakes stuffed with sweet bean paste—while children waited in front.

And then next door to that, with a signboard that had the name "Sagamiya" painted in large letters on it, was a tofu shop. It was Uragawa's house.

In front of the store two or three women who looked like customers were standing. Not sure if it was okay to go inside, Copper stood behind them and waited for a while.

Attending to the patrons in the store was a large woman, about forty years old, with her hair done up in the style called *kushimaki*—a twisted bun fastened with pins and a comb. She had her sleeves rolled up above her elbows, and she, too, was wearing an apron. For some reason aprons seemed really popular in this alley. This woman's apron seemed even now ready to burst open, only just barely managing to wrap itself around her large body. She was sturdy and heavyset, just like a sumo wrestler, with a ruddy complexion.

"Right, one block of cold fresh tofu!" The woman spoke with a voice strong as a man's, putting the tofu into a blue-painted pot, and offered it to the customer. The granny in front of Copper took this and, wrapping it in a large cloth, left the shop with her back hunched against the cold.

"Next—two sheets of fried tofu! Coming up!" The shopkeeper, again speaking in a hearty voice, handed over the fried tofu wrapped in newspaper and received some copper coins in return from a young woman. At that time, she spied Copper's small form, and dropping the coins into the till with a clink, she immediately raised her voice.

"That young man there—whose child is he?"

Caught unawares by her strong voice, Copper was flustered.

"Ah . . . um . . . is Uragawa here?"

The woman looked down at Copper with a surprised expression and then, seeming to understand, nodded her head two or three times.

"Ah, you're a friend of our Tomé, is that it? I thought you were an errand boy from somewhere. Yes, yes, he's here." She turned toward the back of the store and in a loud voice said, "Tomé! A friend is here to see you!"

In the dim recesses at the back of the store, someone was working with his back toward Copper. At the shopkeeper's voice, he turned around in surprise.

It was Uragawa.

"Oh! Honda?"

Uragawa came forward, but when Copper saw him, he was seized with astonishment.

In a neighborhood of so many aprons, perhaps it should have been no surprise that even Uragawa was wearing one. Peeking out from underneath were the same old baggy trousers, and on his feet were a pair of flat-bottomed wooden sandals. As he looked at Uragawa standing there with a pair of long bamboo cooking chopsticks in his hands, Copper's eyes widened in surprise and he spoke.

"You . . . you aren't sick?"

Uragawa hesitated and didn't reply. The big woman replied for him.

"That's right—he's not exactly sick, but one of the boys in the shop is out with a cold, you see. And his father is away, and we're shorthanded, so he's getting a little time off from school! We're so busy right now that sending a note to school—well, we just let that slide. But it's good you're here. Well, well, come right on in!"

Copper and Uragawa entered the back of the shop and sat down on the threshold. With a "Heave ho!" the woman lifted a large brass hibachi and placed it next to Copper, putting some tea on and setting it out.

However, she didn't stay with them long. The customers were calling again.

Sitting there right next to Uragawa, Copper didn't know what to talk about. So he sipped his hot tea, blowing on it to cool it down. Uragawa, too, seemed shy, but presently, stumbling a little over his words, he stood up and said, "Wait just one minute, okay? I have a little more work to do."

In the corner of the shop was a large kettle, as well as an iron pot filled with boiling oil.

"I'm almost done! I just have to fry these—"

Uragawa pointed with his bamboo chopsticks at the stand next to him. Arranged there were four or five thinly sliced pieces of fresh tofu. These he lowered gently into the pot, so as not to break them. Once they were fried, he removed them with the bamboo chopsticks. For the first time Copper was learning how fried tofu was made.

"If I don't cook them now, see, they won't be ready to sell this evening," said Uragawa while watching the pot. And then, with practiced hands, he set about finishing up the fried tofu in the pot. Grasping each piece of deep-fried tofu with the tips of his long bamboo chopsticks, he lifted it from the pot, gave it a little shake to remove the extra oil, and with a little flip tossed it onto a wire rack close by.

Then, while he was waiting for the next piece to finish frying in the pot, he grabbed the ones that were waiting on the rack and—one, two, three—flipped them on their sides, stacking them together and occasionally tapping them lightly with the flat sides of the long chopsticks. When everything was cooked and drained, the finished tofu was all arranged neatly in order.

"Wow!" Copper burst out in admiration. Until this very moment, he had never imagined that Uragawa, who was so hopeless in every kind of physical activity during gym class, could handle those long chopsticks with such dexterity.

Standing in front of the frying pot, Uragawa was the very picture of a tradesman. At that moment, he seemed to Copper as calm and experienced as a seasoned ballplayer with five or six league tournaments under his belt, now taking his turn at the plate.

"Wow!" said Copper again, and at last he managed to

put his admiration into words. "It's really cool that you can do that."

Uragawa smiled in his characteristic way, embarrassed but a little proud.

"How long did you have to practice that?" Copper asked.

"Practice?"

"Uh, I mean, because you're really good."

"I don't practice! I just, you know, help my mom sometimes. But if you make a mistake, it costs like three sen. So naturally I try really hard to get it right . . ."

After he had fried up the remaining four or five slices of tofu, Uragawa called out, "Mom, it's all done!"

"Is it? Thank you! You worked hard." The woman came tripping over in mincing steps that belied her large body and, seizing the pot with a dampened cloth—"Heave ho!"—removed it from the fire. Again, Copper was impressed by her immense strength.

Uragawa removed his apron and blotted his hands with some newspaper that sat nearby. And suddenly there in front of Copper was the same old Uragawa from school.

"Tomé, you two probably have lots to talk about. Why don't you take him to your room?" the woman said to Uragawa. When Uragawa hesitated, the woman addressed Copper in a loud voice.

"Hey, boy—go on back with him. I don't know why, but this child is always worrying about school. The house is a mess, but go ahead and take a look. Well, Tomé, give him the tour. Anyway, I'm sure you've seen enough pretty houses in your life already, right?"

So up they went, climbing the creaky stairs at the back of the shop, to the room where Uragawa studied.

It was a humble north-facing room the size of three tatami mats, about fifteen square meters.

There was a wide bay window of frosted glass, but the topmost pane was transparent, and through it they could just catch a glimpse of the steely-blue winter sky. Outside, they could hear the wind moan, and the glass door shook constantly, rattling in the wind.

On a desk by the window were a notebook, some books, and Uragawa's familiar satchel. The two of them laid out a pair of thin cushions next to the desk and sat on them, facing each other. Then they warmed their hands from both sides of a Seto hibachi, a ceramic fire bowl with glowing coals inside. Uragawa's hands were red from exposure to the cold, and one of the knuckles of his pointer finger had a large red crack in it.

"Do you know when final exams start?" asked Uragawa.

"They said from the seventeenth on."

"Have they already posted the schedule?"

"Nope, not yet. But everyone is saying they'll know this Monday."

Hearing this, Uragawa made a miserable, worried face.

"What page are we up to in English?"

"The end of chapter sixteen."

"And math?"

"We started proportions today!"

Japanese, history, geography, science—Uragawa went over all the subjects one after another, intently asking how far they had advanced during his absence.

Copper worked through Uragawa's textbooks, showing him how far they'd advanced in each subject, one by one. Uragawa put a mark in each section, counting the number of new pages over and over again. He was so worried that Copper started to feel bad for him.

"Hey, it'll be okay. It's only five days—you'll catch up quick!"

"Maybe. But I have no free time during the day, and at night I get sleepy . . ."

"Then let's just do it now—that'll be easiest. We'll just do it in baby steps, little by little, until we're done."

"Well, that's easy for you to say, because you're smart." Uragawa gave a wan smile. Day after day, Uragawa had been waking up before dawn and working together with his entire household to help make the tofu, then rushing hurriedly off to school. That was why at around noon every day, no matter what he did, he would get drowsy and nod off during class.

Then, at times like this, with his father away and one of the workers out sick and the other still learning the ropes, he had to work three times as hard as usual in order to run the store with his mother. He was still a child and not particularly strong, but Uragawa knew how the job was done, and so he was needed to train the new recruit.

Still, exams were approaching, he had put off his studies, and when he thought of school, Uragawa was desperately worried.

Copper was worried, too. "When can you come back to school?" he asked.

"When Papa comes home, I can go right back."

"Will your father be back pretty soon?"

"I don't know. Actually he was supposed to come home the day before yesterday, but . . ."

Copper wondered where Uragawa's father was and why his return was delayed. When he asked, Uragawa hesitated, but then little by little, he explained.

According to Uragawa, his father had gone to his hometown up north, in rural Yamagata prefecture. This was also where Uragawa's mother was born, and Uragawa had many uncles and aunts who lived there.

Copper thought it was funny that Uragawa's family called their store Sagamiya even though they came from

Yamagata, on the other side of the country, but Uragawa explained that it was because his father had originally worked in the shop and then inherited the name from the previous owners when he went into business for himself.

His father's situation was that he was trying to raise money. Uragawa didn't know if it was hundreds of yen or less than that. Why he needed the money was also a mystery. But in any case, if his father didn't get it now, it would be a big problem. That was why he went to consult with Uragawa's uncles way up in the Yamagata country-side, where the snow was already really deep.

The fact that he wasn't back surely meant that he was having unexpected trouble raising the money. That was all Uragawa knew about it, but just knowing that was enough to unsettle him. As he was telling the story, little by little, a dark shadow stole over Uragawa's childlike face. Somehow it made him look like an adult.

"But listen, don't tell anyone about this, okay? Because my mom thinks I don't know," Uragawa said in a low voice. "The night before my dad left, I was up all night. So I heard my dad and my mom talking about it."

Copper tried to think of what to say to console Uragawa, but he couldn't find the words. It was an oppressive feeling beyond compare. He had never felt anything in his life that weighed upon his heart like this.

He felt bad for Uragawa, but what could Copper do?

If Uragawa was that seriously worried, how could a few superficial words make him feel better?

Copper was silent, gazing at the glowing coal embers in the hibachi. The window rattled with a clickety-clack, and the wind's incessant howling outside echoed terribly in Copper's ears.

"Really, please don't tell anyone, okay?" Uragawa said after a little while.

"I would never do that!" Copper replied, feeling like he had been rescued. Even if his reply was only of limited consolation to Uragawa, it helped Copper a lot. Without Uragawa's knowing, the words raised Copper's spirits.

"I won't say anything. I promise. We can pinky-swear."

Copper held out his hand with the little finger extended. He felt he would promise anything if only it would make Uragawa happy.

Uragawa's frostbitten red pinky hooked together with Copper's little finger. The two of them tugged hard on their fingers to cement the bond. As they did, both of their faces turned serious.

This was particularly true for Uragawa, who was bearing the pain in his frostbitten finger with a tightened jaw, but when they released their grip and the fingers fell apart, they looked at each other and smiled in spite of themselves.

Uragawa's face was full of trust for Copper.

Then briefly, coming from down the hall, they heard a weak cough: "Ahem! Ahem!"

"Right, right—I have to look in on Kichi-don," Uragawa murmured. "He works here. He caught a cold and he's sleeping. I'm just going to check on him, okay?"

Then, just as Uragawa was about to get up, the heavy paper-covered *fusuma* door between the rooms slid open, and Copper was startled to see a boy who couldn't have been more than six years old. Behind him stood a girl who looked to be in fifth or sixth grade, respectfully holding out a tray with tea and a dish of sweets.

The boy wore a jacket and trousers made of wool, and had a round face just like Uragawa, only with narrow eyes, like two small cracks in the skin of his face. His cheeks and his hands and his jacket were all fearfully dirty. The girl was carrying a baby bound up on her back, and she, too, was dressed all in wool, in the Western style.

The boy just stood there, staring boldly at Copper, but the girl came in with small graceful steps, bearing the tray.

Surely she was thinking this must be the perfect opportunity to put into practice the formal etiquette that she had learned in school. With a ferociously calm look on her face, she advanced toward them, step by step, looking exactly as if she were the class valedictorian advancing to receive her diploma at the podium.

When she arrived in front of Copper, she knelt down, bowed politely, presented the tray, and again bowed. In the dish on the tray were the sweet bean *taiyaki* cakes from the shop next door, steaming hot.

"Your younger sister?" Copper asked Uragawa.

"Yes. And that's my little brother."

Uragawa's sister stood up and executed a crisp about-face—one, two, three—and left the room, walking as carefully as when she came, but then took a hurried glance in the direction of her younger brother, who was still standing stock-still.

"Bun-chan! What are you doing?" she called out. "You're so awful! Bad manners. Come on—get over here!"

Before anyone knew what was happening, the boy had entered the room and was again riveted, standing there staring at the sweet bean cakes. From the looks of him, not a word that his sister spoke was entering his ears.

"Come on! I said, let's go! You're such a pain!"

The girl tried to grab her younger brother's hand, but Bun-chan batted her hand away and resumed gazing at the bean cakes with some intensity.

Taking a cake from the dish, Copper offered it to the boy. The boy took a quick glance at Copper's face, then silently accepted the cake and immediately put it in his mouth. His older sister was already utterly furious with him.

"Really, you're terrible! You have no manners. I'm taking you to mother, and we'll see what happens." She took Bun-chan's hand and, with a tug, pulled him from the room. Bun-chan, cheeks full of cake, allowed himself to be dragged out.

"My sister is head of her class. She's better at school than me," Uragawa said.

After that, the two of them had cake. This was the first time Copper had ever eaten *taiyaki*. Copper's mother never let him eat junk food. Because he had been told so often that eating such foods would hurt his stomach, Copper himself had never thought he wanted to eat them.

But when he actually tasted it, perhaps because he was so hungry, he thought it was delicious.

"Ahem! Ahem!" Again the weak cough found its way to them.

"Oh, that's right—I was going to check on Kichi-don . . ." Leaving his half-eaten cake on the tray, Uragawa asked Copper to excuse him for a moment and left the room.

Shortly after Uragawa stepped out, from the direction of the room where it seemed the sick person was sleeping, Copper could hear voices in whispered conversation.

". . . Isn't that true? So it's fine." That was Uragawa's voice speaking. Something was fine, but he couldn't hear the other person.

"It's okay, so you should just sleep. I can . . ." It appeared Uragawa was diligently trying to persuade the sick person to rest. And then there was the sound of a *fusuma* door sliding, and Copper could tell from the clatter coming from down the hall that Uragawa had started to do something. Copper stood up, slid open the door of the room he was in, and peered down the hallway in the direction of the noise.

At the bend in the dim corridor, Uragawa was crouched, using a pick to hack with all his strength at a chunk of ice that had been placed in a washbasin. At Uragawa's feet, lying limply on its side, was an ice pack in which the ice had all melted into water.

For the sake of the ailing Kichi-don, Uragawa was refreshing the ice in the pack.

"I have to go home now," said Copper at around three o'clock in the afternoon.

Before that, he had turned to Uragawa and made him a second promise. He promised that on the coming Tuesday, he would come to Uragawa's house again, to teach him any parts of the English and math that he didn't understand, and also that he would lend him his own notes to study with before the exams.

Uragawa, in turn, had promised that when Copper

came next time, Uragawa would let him run the motor that they had in the shop.

Along the wall of the shop, in a space of only about two square meters, Uragawa's family had set up a machine to grind soybeans for the tofu. The machine was designed so that a leather belt powered by a motor would spin a stone mill round and round with a thunderous noise. Uragawa thought that as a thank-you to Copper, he would let him run the machine with his own hands.

Copper was, of course, immensely grateful. The only motor Copper had was a toy one, bought at the department store, and it didn't compare in any way with the real thing.

"My goodness, going already?"

Uragawa's mother was standing in the shop as before, attending to her customers, but when she saw Copper leaving, she addressed him again in her strong voice.

"We were a little busy today, but don't let that scare you off, okay? Unlike you, young man, our Tomé isn't such an easy talker, but he was very happy to see you today. Isn't that right, Tomé?"

With a self-conscious smile, Uragawa nodded silently.

But not a minute later, a greater happiness arrived for Uragawa.

Copper was about to head home, and Uragawa was following him out to see him off, when at that moment, like a bird dropping out of the sky, a red bicycle stopped at the storefront, and the young man riding it hopped nimbly off.

"Telegram for Uragawa!"

I scarcely need to tell you that it was a telegram from Uragawa's father in Yamagata prefecture. Uragawa quickly realized that and fixed his eyes on his mother's face as she opened and read the telegram. He would know from her expression whether the telegram contained good news or bad.

What sort of face would it be? With bated breath, Copper, too, pinned his eyes to the large woman's face.

Brows knit, she examined the telegram, and then, when she had finished reading, she broke into a smile. With a sigh, the two boys breathed again. On the woman's face, too, there was an unmistakable tinge of relief.

"Tomé, this evening your father is coming home. At last!" And she handed the telegram to Uragawa.

On the telegram, in light-purple letters, the following was written:

TALK DONE HOME TONIGHT

The two of them went outside. Under the strip of clear sky visible from the narrow street, the cold wind swept over the rooftops, howling as before. Copper and Uragawa, shoulder to shoulder, made their way along the tunnel of the alley to the train station, dodging the press of the crowd as they walked. Uragawa seemed not to notice the passersby.

"Hey, when it said 'talk done' . . ." Uragawa asked quietly.

"That? It probably means that your uncles said yes."

"And that's it."

"Definitely."

"That's it. Okay, that must be it."

The two of them talked together excitedly.

This meant that Uragawa could stop worrying and that he would be able to go to school. As they walked, Uragawa gathered momentum step by step, and his happiness became readily apparent. If only he could go to school, Uragawa wouldn't even mind being teased and made fun of again.

At the end of the alley, when they came as far as the corner that let out onto the boulevard, the two of them parted.

"Well, see you . . ." Uragawa said, sad to say goodbye, and headed back along the heavily aproned street.

Copper walked rapidly along the boulevard where the harsh wind played, sometimes covering his face to avoid the wind. Somehow there was an extra spring in his step.

The following Tuesday, as promised, Copper visited Uragawa once more.

The conversation they had at that time was a long one, but to be brief, Uragawa was able to catch up on all his missed schoolwork, thanks to Copper, and for the moment have some peace of mind. And Copper being who he was, nothing could have topped his satisfaction at being able to operate the switch that ran the motor in the tofu shop.

Taken with Copper's delight in the hum of the motor as it spun, Uragawa's mother—that large woman from the shop—looked on in deep admiration, hands on her hips and elbows spread wide.

This boy, well, he's a different story from us, she must have been thinking.

Back at home, Copper bolted a late dinner, and although he was told that it was already eight o'clock, he set out for his uncle's house.

His uncle was warming himself under a quilt at the low, heated table called a *kotatsu*, and reading the evening edition of the newspaper with the lights dimmed, but had he settled in too soon? There was Copper's voice at the door.

"Uncle, today I ran a motor!" he boasted, without any delay.

"A motor, you say? Was it your toy?"

"Don't be ridiculous! It was the real thing. I ran a genuine motor!"

"Well! A grand thing, isn't that? Where in the world did you find a real motor?"

Asked in such a way, Copper suddenly felt it could be embarrassing to answer that, well, it was a motor in a tofu shop. So after a brief silence, the uncle tried once more.

"Did you go to a factory somewhere?"

"Ye–es."

"What sort of factory?"

"A certain food-product manufacturing plant!" Copper replied in an important voice.

"Food product, you say? What was it?"

"It was—well, it started with soybeans as a raw material . . ."

"And then?"

"And then boiling that . . ."

"And after that?"

"Then grinding that up . . ."

Having listened thus far, the uncle grinned and let out a laugh. Then, picking up where Copper left off, he continued on his own.

". . . And after an appropriate amount of time, put it in a basket, steam it, cut it into white blocks two and a half centimeters thick, seven and a half centimeters wide, and fifteen centimeters long . . . Is that it? After immersing it in water to cool it, sell it at five sen per block . . . Something like that?"

"Darn! You guessed it."

Copper rubbed his head in embarrassment. His uncle laughed, but soon enough his face turned straight again.

"You went to Uragawa's house, I gather?" he asked.

Copper told his uncle of the two visits.

Everything that he had seen and heard at Uragawa's house was completely new to Copper. It would be lots of fun to tell his uncle about it.

"The lady at Uragawa's place—Uncle, she's tremendous. Just like Tamanishiki, the sumo champion. Because there was a pot full of oil that was this big, and she said 'Heave ho!' and lifted it right up, all by herself. Uncle, I think she might even be stronger than you!"

"Well! She does sound tremendous, indeed. If I were careless enough to go into Uragawa's house, I'm sure she'd pluck me up and toss me right out."

"No, if you don't do anything wrong there, you'll be fine. She's really nice! I like her."

Asked by his uncle, Copper related the story of Uragawa and his house in detail. Except when it came to Uragawa's father going all the way to Yamagata to raise money, he didn't say a thing. Copper was definitely keeping his promise.

After listening to the story, his uncle said, "You and your friends are different from Uragawa in many ways—do you see that? So it's not unreasonable that he would have trouble fitting in with everyone. By the way, I have something I'd like you to think about . . ."

"What is it?"

"What do you think is the greatest difference between all of you and Uragawa?"

"The greatest difference . . . Hmm." Copper looked a little confused. Then he hesitated a while but presently, with some difficulty, spoke.

"Uh, Uragawa's family is—well, they're poor. But our family isn't."

"Exactly." His uncle nodded and asked again, "But leaving aside the comparison of the two families, what differences do you think there might be between Uragawa himself and you?"

"Well . . ." Copper was at a bit of a loss as to how to respond.

At that time the clock reached nine thirty and rang once for the half hour. Tomorrow was a school day, and Copper wasn't allowed to stay up so late at night. So Copper and his uncle had to break off their discussion midway through, and Copper ran home in a great hurry.

But his uncle's last question held within it a problem of some importance. This evening, too, his uncle wrote intently in the notebook after Copper went home. So let's take another peek into that notebook and see what's written there.

On Poverty and Humanity

~~~~~~

(I)

Copper,

You have been kind to Uragawa in different ways, and that is a very good thing.

He has often been excluded by your classmates, and your visits must have made him quite happy.

And if you think about how your own deeds were able to make a poor, lonely friend so happy, that is surely a fine feeling for you as well.

What's more, to learn that Uragawa, who has been teased by everyone, has a beautiful spirit and kind feelings, nothing to be ridiculed at all—well, that was a valuable experience for you.

Listening to your story, I was very impressed by what you did and said. You didn't think of yourself as the least bit superior to Uragawa or put yourself on a higher level, but that is no doubt because you and Uragawa are both good, honest people.

If Uragawa had not been such a nice young man, you might have thought, *Well, it's because he's so bad at school.* No, there's even a chance that deep inside, even if you didn't say it out loud, you might have thought something like *Well, it's because he's poor.*

One reason you didn't feel that way is that Uragawa has a kind and honest nature.

But on the other hand, say you were to brag about your good grades, hold Uragawa's family in contempt for their poverty, and so forth—you can be sure that he wouldn't take any pleasure from your kindness.

I am truly happy that neither of you were at all like that.

In particular, I am happier than you can know that you have not an ounce of contempt within you for the poverty of Uragawa's family.

Copper, as you make your way toward adulthood, you will eventually come to understand that to lead a life of poverty is often to go about one's life feeling inferior to others.

It's easy to catch oneself feeling ashamed of one's shabby clothes, squalid home, or coarse food.

Of course there are also magnificent people who take rightful pride in themselves as they live their lives, despite the fact that they are poor. But many in this world seem to lose their self-respect in the presence of the wealthy and instead bow and scrape blindly, as if they wonder whether they are complete equals. These people, of course, deserve contempt. Not because they have no money. It's because their servile nature allows no alternative.

But Copper, even those who have all due self-respect may feel small at times if they're living in poverty. It's an inevitable part of human nature. And we don't want to cause needless embarrassment to people, so we must not forget to make a habit of modesty and restraint in our lives. Human beings should never be so humiliated as to damage their self-respect. But people who live in poverty are often forced to endure such indignities, so we must remember that their pride can be easily wounded.

So in theory, then, saying that someone is poor shouldn't make them feel small. It should go without saying that the true worth of a person doesn't depend on that person's clothes or house or food. No matter what kind of magnificent garments they wear or grand mansion they inhabit, fools are fools, boors are boorish, and their value as people shouldn't be elevated for those reasons. Furthermore, if someone has a noble mind and great insight, then we owe it to them to respect them as great, even if they are impoverished.

Therefore, someone with true confidence in their value as a human being should be able to live unaffected, even if their circumstances shift a bit this way or that.

You and I, too, because we are human, must live with only our value as human beings in mind, not thinking we are unimportant if we happen to be poor or that we are great because we lead a wealthy life.

Someone who feels inferior because they are poor can never be much of a human being.

Still, just because we must always be ready to look at ourselves that way, that doesn't mean it's okay to ignore the fragile spirits of those in poverty.

At least, Copper, until the day that you have stood in the place of the poor and tasted the bitter pain of poverty and then stood up to the world time and again, without losing your confidence, you are not qualified to do so.

Please hold this thought deep in your heart.

If you were to start to feel even a little proud of your family's good life and to look down on people less wealthy than you, more thoughtful souls would be right to laugh at you. Because a human being who doesn't understand the essentials of being human, in other words, is a pitiful fool.

Of course, you went to Uragawa's house and didn't act like you were above him in the slightest. I know full well that right now you would never look down on the poor. However, what you still don't know is how important it is to hold on to that attitude as you become an adult.

But I think I will take this opportunity to let you know just how important it is. The better you understand the world, the more important this will become. Or, rather, its importance is something you must never forget if you want to understand the world properly at all.

As for why this is so—please remember this well—it's because in the world today, the vast majority of people are poor. So the vast majority of the people in this world are unable to live their lives in a way that is really human—this is the problem of our time, greater than any other.

(II)

You visited Uragawa's house and saw the differences between the Uragawa household and yours. You know that compared to yours, Uragawa's house is the poorer of the two.

However, you may be shocked to learn how many people in the world can't even live the life the Uragawas have! To these people, the Uragawa family is anything but poor.

As a matter of fact, consider the young people who are working for the Uragawa family. How long will those people labor with nothing but the dream of having a shop like the Uragawas?

Although we say the Uragawas are poor, they send their son to junior high school. But their young employees must give up their education after elementary school.

Furthermore, the Uragawa family makes a living out of their own home, running a business with the tofu machine installed there, buying raw soybeans, and hiring young employees. Meanwhile, those employees have not a single thing to support themselves other than their own labor. They live from day to day on the work of their bodies.

If, by chance, people such as these came down with a chronic illness or found themselves unable to work due to a serious injury, what in the world would they do? If you rely on your own labor to live, then not to be able to work is to face starvation, is it not?

Despite that, the sad truth is that in today's world, the people who will be in the most trouble if they get hurt are the people who are in the greatest danger of getting hurt.

Poor-quality food, unsanitary living conditions, and on top of that, work day after day. Even the hope that the next day will bring freedom from exhaustion is an inconceivable luxury. In such a life one is pursued by work constantly.

Do you remember last summer, when we went with your mother to the Bōshū seashore? The train pulled out of the station at Ryōgoku, and for a while we surveyed the countryside from above on the elevated line. The Honjo and Jōtō wards were bristling with smokestacks big and small, sticking up row upon row like a forest, emitting thick clouds of smoke. Under the blinding-hot summer sky, the dense-packed rooftops stretched on without a gap, and the countless smoking chimneys continued faintly all the way to the horizon. The hot wind passing above blew the smoke all the way into the train.

The moment we left Ryōgoku, you were saying that you wanted ice cream. Do you remember?

But at the same time that we decided we could no longer endure the heat of Tokyo and departed for the seashore, dozens or perhaps hundreds of laborers were working under each of those roofs, sweaty and dusty.

And then we had left the city behind, and we were gazing across the wide-open blue-green fields, and at last we felt that cool breeze and breathed a sigh of relief. But when you think about it, all those lush green rice paddies were built with the hard labor of peasants who could never escape on a summer holiday.

Actually, when you looked through the train windows, weren't there any number of peasants, even women, scattered here and there, diligently weeding the rice paddies, up to their hips in water?

These sorts of people exist. They are anywhere you go in Japan—no, anywhere you go in the world, they form the greatest part of the population.

Every day, these people must endure all sorts of hardships. In a life in which there's never quite enough of anything, it's hard even to get treatment for an illness.

Moreover, consider both the culture that is our pride and the masterworks of art and music that bring us joy. For such people, these are wishes not to be granted.

Copper! You have read both volumes of *How Many Things Have Human Beings Done?* You know the glorious history of human struggle. How for tens of thousands of years we piled effort upon effort to advance at last from our primitive life in ancient times to our current civilization.

But today, the fruits of those labors are not awarded to everyone.

I'm sure you are saying, *That can't be right.*

You're correct. It's wrong for sure. We are all human beings, so if we can't all live a life that is really human, something is wrong. A society that doesn't allow that is wrong. Nobody can deny this, as long as they have an honest heart.

Today, no matter how shameful it seems, our society is not there yet. One might say the human race has progressed, but we still haven't made it that far. This remains a problem for now and the days to come.

After all, how much suffering has poverty caused in our world? How many people have been sunk in misery? How many deep-rooted conflicts have been seeded?

You have such a happy life now that I don't want to have this conversation with you. But even if I don't explain, you will eventually learn it to be true, no matter what you do.

So why, in a society of such advanced civilization as ours, does such a repugnant state of affairs remain in existence? Why has such misery not been eradicated in this world?

This, too, will be hard to comprehend at your age. For the most part, if you read the "Society" chapter in *A Guide to Human Life*, you will understand, but as you get older and know more of complex social relationships, and your judgment, too, matures, if you can come to a correct conclusion about this, it won't be too late.

For now, what I want you to understand clearly is what a gift it is, in a society like this, to be able to study unhindered, as you do, and to be able to expand your abilities as you wish. In Japanese, we might call it *arigatai*.

Copper! Pay careful attention to the word *arigatai*. As you know, we use it to express thanks or gratitude. But the root of the word in Japanese means something more like "difficult," "hard," or "impossible." It means "this never happens."

We are grateful for good fortune specifically because we feel that it rarely happens. Thus, the word *arigatai* has come to refer to something special or rare enough to be thankful for. So when we say *arigatou*, or thank you, in Japanese, it becomes an expression of gratitude.

If you survey the whole wide world and then on top of that look back at yourself now, you would probably describe your present state as *arigatai*, wouldn't you?

Just because a person graduated from elementary school like you, it doesn't mean they can attend junior high school the way you do. And if they are in a home like Uragawa's, they must take time off from studying to work.

On the other hand, you have nothing interfering with your studies. And through those studies, you are free to take anything you wish from the accumulated results of tens of thousands of years of human efforts.

If you do—

No, I think you will understand without me saying anything more. I expect you will know perfectly well what one must do, what the true goals in life are, when a person stands in such a fortunate place as you do.

Together with your late father and with your mother, who hangs a lifetime of hope on you, I pray from my heart—

That you extend your talents in leaps and bounds and become a person truly useful to the world!

Please, Copper!

(III)

One final thing: I'll pose a question for you, so please think it over.

Through your "human net" theory, you know well by now how closely we are all tied to our fellow beings.

People working in great hardship and those of us living in relative happiness are completely cut off from each other in our daily lives, but actually we are bound together by an unbreakable net.

So if we don't care about those people and we live thinking only of our own happiness, that is wrong, is it not?

But even if we agree that we must consider those people, it would be a terrible mistake to look at things only from the perspective of the unfortunate, the pitiful, or those who deserve sympathy.

Copper, there's another thing there that must not be overlooked.

Think of those who had to stop school early to support themselves through labor. Clearly, there are many among them, even adults, who don't know what you know. It's normal for such people to have only a very basic level of knowledge of things that are not taught outside school, such as geometry, algebra, and physics. Their tastes can be working-class as well.

If you look at things only from this viewpoint, it's not impossible that you might see yourself as superior to these people. But when you try changing your point of view, these people are the very ones bearing this entire world on their shoulders. They are fantastic people beyond comparison to those such as yourself.

Think this over. Of all the things that all of us need to live, every one is the product of human labor, is it not?

Even for the most lofty work in the arts and sciences, all we need is created by such people, by the sweat of their brow.

Without the labor of those people, we would have no civilization, and without that, there would be no progress for society.

And what about you? What will you create? You take many things from the world, but I wonder what you will give back in return?

You use things without thinking twice about it, but at the same time, you still haven't created a thing.

Three meals a day, sweets, the pencil you use to study, ink, pen, paper—you are still in school, but every day, you consume a great number of things in your life. Clothes, shoes, furniture like your desk, and the house you live in, too—because these things will all wear out eventually, you are using them as well, little by little, in installments.

From that perspective, we could say your daily life is the life of an expert consumer, could we not?

Of course, ultimately, nobody can live without food and clothing, so nobody just produces things and doesn't consume anything. And the reason we make things in the first place is so that they can be used, so you can't say that consuming things is bad in and of itself.

But between the people who produce things over and above what they consume, and send them out into the world, and the people who don't produce anything and who do nothing but consume, which are the great human beings? Which are the important human beings? If you ask yourself this, it's not much of a puzzle, is it?

If nobody made anything, there would be no tastes, no pleasures—consumption would be impossible. The work of making things itself makes it possible for people to be truly human. This is not just a matter of food and clothing. In the academic world, in the art world, the producers are needed far more than the consumers.

Try not to overlook this point of difference between producers and consumers. When you look at things from this point, you're certain to find a surprising number of utterly worthless people living in magnificent mansions and riding in their cars with their big heads held high. And you'll find, too, among those who are most often looked down upon, that there are many people to whom we should bow our own heads.

So then, Copper, this may be the greatest difference between you and Uragawa!

Uragawa is still young in years, but if we think about who makes things for the world, couldn't we say he is already a great person? The smell of fried tofu that has seeped into his clothes—even if Uragawa doesn't brag about it, it's certainly no shame.

Which is to say that you may feel scolded for being a consumer and not producing anything, but that was never my intention. You and your friends are all still students, still preparing to stand on your own in the world, so for now, that doesn't matter.

Only, you are, for the moment, expert consumers, so you must understand that for now, this is your station in life. You and your classmates ought to have humble respect for Uragawa, who, even if he can't change his station, has, without complaint, taken on a great responsibility in helping with his family's business.

To mock that from your social position, even for a moment, is to not know your own place and is a great error.

So learn just that, and learn it well, and on top of that, there is one more thing I'd like you to consider.

When you think of the things you need in your daily life, you don't produce any of them, so you are definitely a consumer. But while you may not have noticed, there is something else, a big thing that you produce day after day. What could that be?

Copper, I choose not to tell you the answer to this problem, because I'd like you to find an answer to it yourself.

There's no particular need to hurry. If you don't forget, you'll find an answer in your own good time.

But you must never ask anyone else.

Because you'll never know if someone else's answer makes sense for you or not. It's necessary to find it for yourself.

The answer may come to you suddenly, even tomorrow maybe. Or else you may reach adulthood and still not know. But I believe that everyone must find this answer at some point in their life, because we are all human.

Anyway, please fix this question in your mind, and remember it sometimes, and think it over well. Surely a day will come when it will be worth your while.

That's it for now, but mind you, don't forget!

~~~~~~

Chapter Five

Napoleon and the Four Young Men

The large Western-style mansion where Mizutani lived stood on a hill in Takanawa, overlooking the Shinagawa sea. The hill was covered with dense groves of trees even though it was winter, and the estate was surrounded by an iron fence, with a weather vane perched high atop its slate-covered roof. One could easily imagine the old-fashioned mansion to be a relic of the Meiji era, when Western styles became popular in Japan, a century before, and surrounded by garden trees and shrubs as it was, there was a hush anytime one went there.

On the fifth day of the new year, Copper visited Mizutani at this house for the first time in a long while.

That day, they were expecting Kitami and Uragawa as well. The second-term exams were safely behind them, the results had been posted, and just before their long-awaited winter vacation commenced, Mizutani had invited Copper and his two friends to come play.

Copper had visited Mizutani's house any number of times since elementary school, but this was a first for Kitami and Uragawa. In truth, Uragawa was invited because, after hearing his story from Copper, Mizutani suddenly began to be friendly to him.

Speaking of the second-term exam results, Copper had received top marks as usual. What's more, Uragawa's grades had improved unexpectedly from the previous semester, and he himself was particularly pleased with his English scores. Copper's support had clearly been effective.

Both Copper and Uragawa were feeling good about the new year.

So the fact that his three close friends were getting together was especially fun for Copper. It was a bright, sunny afternoon, with the wind unusually still for winter in Tokyo, and Copper hastened toward Mizutani's house, through streets lined with the large woven-straw *kadomatsu* planters that signified the holiday season, full of pine and bamboo, set in pairs flanking every doorway of the well-to-do residential neighborhood.

By the broad stacked-stone gateposts of Mizutani's house, two of these ceremonial pine trees stood as tall as adults, like an honor guard presenting arms. Inside the gate, an ancient chinquapin tree towered, blotting out the sky with its deep shade. Circling under that, a gravel path climbed up toward the house, where it ended in front of a magnificent entrance with a covered porch. On the round grass lawn in front of the entrance, four or five fat palm trees rubbed their shaggy trunks together, fronds spreading like fingers in all directions as they soaked up the sun that was shining over the roof of the tall mansion.

Usually the heavy door was shut, but today the silent entryway was thrown wide open, and a box had been placed in front to collect visitors' calling cards.

I wonder if Kitami and the rest of them are already here? Copper pressed the front doorbell.

A young steward came out. When he saw Copper's face, he said, "Ah, please come in. Everyone has gathered, and they are waiting for you."

As Copper took off his shoes to enter the house, he noticed a pair of rough, thick-soled work boots and a pair of soccer shoes lined up neatly next to each other off to the side, on the ground under an exquisite potted pine.

Copper followed the steward down a dark carpeted corridor full of twists and turns. When Copper came to

Mizutani's place, he always thought, *Wow, what a big house.* He wondered what anyone would do with so many different rooms.

But the steward walked on in front of him without a word. There was nothing for Copper to do but hurry after him in silence.

Mizutani's room was in a separate building that they called the annex. This was a newly constructed area made specially for Mizutani and his siblings, built of glass and reinforced concrete so that lots of sunlight could enter everywhere. From every room, Copper could see the vast sweep of Shinagawa Bay below.

Mizutani's father was a person who represented people of great influence in the business world. Directors, auditors, presidents of large companies and banks from all over—you couldn't count all the important titles on both hands. As a man of means, he thought he'd like to make his children as happy as possible.

The steward arrived at last at Mizutani's room, with Copper in tow, and knocked on the door.

"Come in! Who is it?" replied a lovely voice from inside. Copper remembered this voice. When he opened the door, a figure in a yellow sweater spun lightly around to face him. It was a young lady of seventeen or eighteen, with bobbed hair and clean-cut features. She was Mizutani's older sister. Mizutani, Kitami, and Uragawa were seated in a row by the window with the warm sunlight streaming in, the three of them looking unaccountably well behaved.

"Ah, Copper? You're late, aren't you? We were starting to think you weren't coming." The young woman welcomed Copper, and then greeted him again more formally: "In any case, a happy New Year to you!"

"You too," Copper replied, but he was a little bit surprised. Mizutani's sister was wearing pants, just like he was, even though she was a woman. Even though she must have noticed Copper's wondering look, the young woman continued to talk in a calm and matter-of-fact way.

"It's been a long time, hasn't it? But, Copper, you're still just as small as ever, aren't you?"

"Don't be silly! Compared to last year, I'm five centimeters taller!" Copper protested, mortified. "You're not so big yourself, Katsuko."

"How rude!" she replied teasingly. "I'm ninth in my class—not second to last, like Mr. Somebody."

"Hey! I mean, fine, whatever. People can say what they want," Copper replied, looking resigned. Then he hastily made his way over to Kitami and the others. The three stood up and exchanged New Year's wishes with Copper, and he asked what they had been doing.

"Until you came, we were listening to Mizutani's sister's story," Kitami replied. "It was good! You should listen, too."

Copper settled into a nearby chair. The chair was a stylish one, made of a steel bar bent into shape like a single brushstroke and covered with thick cloth where it met the back and hips. Really, the things in the room—the desk, the bookshelves, the table lamp, everything—were united by their simple, beautiful lines, without the slightest bit of unnecessary ornamentation. The room overflowed with an utterly fresh, bright, modern feeling everywhere. Through the glass windows, one could see the reflection of the sunlight sparkling on the Shinagawa sea.

"Katsuko's story—is it a fairy tale?" asked Copper.

"Oh, please, Copper! I was just now telling them the story of a real-life hero," Katsuko replied.

"Really? Sounds complicated."

"It's not complicated at all. I think everyone should have a heroic spirit, whether they're a man or a woman," said Katsuko, at which point Kitami interjected:

"Then please, will you tell us the rest of the story?"

So Katsuko, standing in front of the four boys, began to speak.

". . . As I was saying, there's a really amazing story from the time of the Battle of Wagram. This was in July of 1809. One side was the army of France, led by Napoleon, and the other side was the combined armies of Austria and Russia, and they met near the Danube River. The fate of the three countries all depended on this one battle, so of course it was a ferocious fight. Even though Napoleon's army was really strong, he was facing the allied armies of two countries at once. It wasn't going to be an easy victory.

"One special thing Russia had was their famous Cossack cavalry. The Cossacks had made raids into Napoleon's territory, time after time, and had almost reached his headquarters! Hundreds of them would come galloping forward all at once, just like a tidal wave, and break through the front lines of the French, trampling the enemy under their horses' feet.

"Napoleon's honor guard—the imperial troops—were fighting desperately against them, and finally they managed to repel them, but every time they thought they'd pushed them back, again and again, a new wave of Cossack soldiers would attack, fighting tooth and nail, in a struggle to the death, over the corpses of their fallen comrades. Even the honor guard—said to be invincible—were themselves at many times in great danger."

Here Katsuko paused to take a breath. Then, surveying her eager listeners, she continued.

"At this time, Napoleon was watching the battle from a hill overlooking the battlefield. Of course, the Cossacks noticed this and began to push in his direction. So Napoleon's advisers, who were standing next to him, began to get nervous.

"'Your Excellency, please evacuate from here, at least for the present.'

"Over and over, they begged him to go. But Napoleon wouldn't leave that dangerous hill. No matter how they begged, he refused to retreat to a safer location.

"Do you all understand why Napoleon refused to leave?" Katsuko placed both hands on her hips and, with her feet planted, waited for an answer from the four boys. But the four boys being who they were, they just made faces as if they didn't know what to say and gazed at Katsuko. At that, she shook her head once, brushed a stray hair from her bangs out of her face, and began to speak animatedly again.

"If it were only about monitoring the battlefield, he could have moved to a safer place! So he wasn't staying just to command his troops. Nothing like that. Napoleon, he watched the Cossack enemy—he watched them with fascination! He couldn't look away.

"'What bravery! What valor!' he said, admiring them as he watched them attacking his own command, again and again. With complete disregard for their own safety . . . Actually, it was wonderful."

Katsuko's eyes were sparkling, and her cheeks had flushed red.

"I really think he's great. Just think about it—it's war! If you lose, your life is on the line! No matter who wins, you or the opponent, it's a fight to the death. And in the middle of that, to praise your enemy—to be enchanted by your enemy's bravery—actually, I think that's awesome. Actually, it's heroic."

Katsuko was excited, and her gaze became dreamy and distant. Copper thought she was beautiful.

"So which side won?" Mizutani asked excitedly. "Napoleon?"

"Well, Hayao, can't you all tell?" Katsuko gave her brother a mock look of surprise. "Of course Napoleon won. After a fierce battle that took two days, Napoleon finally defeated the combined armies of Austria and Russia. But this is not about winners and losers!"

"But losing is bad, isn't it?"

"Oh boy. You just don't get it, do you? Win or lose, heroes are heroes! Actually, real heroes are great even when they lose. Hayao, if you're a man, you should understand this!"

Katsuko tilted her head and frowned sadly. Her hair hung lightly over her face. And then, as if she were thinking of some weighty problem, she jammed both hands in her trouser pockets and began to pace back and forth silently in front of the four boys. Uragawa and Kitami gaped at Katsuko, dumbfounded. Copper and Mizutani glanced at each other.

"Sis, you look like you want to become Napoleon," Mizutani said in a low voice. Copper widened his eyes.

"Of course, going into battle, nobody thinks, *I want to lose*." Katsuko, still pacing, once again started to speak. "Life is important to everyone. Nobody likes getting injured. I've never seen war, but if I were in one, I think I'd probably be totally terrified. Sure, anyone would tremble in fear the first time. But—

"But people can forget their fear if a heroic spirit burns within them. Courage grows in a person, higher than any barrier, and then even your precious life becomes less precious. I think that's the most fantastic thing. People becoming more than people—"

Kitami let out a murmur of admiration.

"But it's not only about not valuing your life! If it were just that, any reckless fool could do it. If someone acts desperate and crazy just to look like a daredevil, that's not a great person! That person's no different from a wild dog. But if a person can go to a place where they can say they no longer need their life, even when they're not desperate or crazy, well, that's what I think is fantastic."

Again, an involuntary noise from Kitami. Next to him, Uragawa, for his part, was looking at Katsuko with equal parts confusion and excitement. He had never met a young woman like this before.

"When I think how sometimes people can be brave enough to overcome any fear, any hardship, it gives me a feeling I can hardly describe. To charge right at the things that are painful and difficult, break through to the other side, and take pleasure in that—don't you think that's truly fantastic? The greater the suffering, the greater the joy in overcoming it. So you don't fear death anymore! I think that's what a heroic spirit is all about.

"I truly believe that to die this way, moved by this kind of spirit, is a way, way greater thing than to live a long but lazy and aimless life. If you lose pierced by this spirit, then it's not a loss. If you win but you are missing this spirit, you can't really call yourself a winner."

At this point Katsuko stopped where she stood, and spoke in a voice overflowing with emotion.

"Oh, just once in my life, I want to go through a great trial and feel it myself! No matter how hard, it would be wonderful. Napoleon is great, isn't he? Because his whole life was ruled by this spirit. He was heroism itself. So he admired the enemy's bravery and couldn't look away. I think that's truly heroic.

"Say, Copper?"

Katsuko suddenly called out Copper's name. Then, taking up a small picture postcard in a stand on the desk, she showed it to him while she spoke.

"Copper, what do you think of this picture?"

It was a picture of Napoleon marching across a wide field at the head of a great army. Spread across the upper half of the picture was the dark, dark winter sky. In a desolate field in which not a single blade of grass could be seen, a thin layer of snow had fallen. A great number of cannons must have recently rolled by—the snow in the road was frozen into deep ruts carved by the impression of their wheels. Napoleon was riding forward along the rough-torn road, astride a beautiful white horse, eyes fixed somewhere off in the distance. Behind him followed many of his generals and staff, similarly mounted. Then in the still-snowy field beyond them, large squads of foot soldiers could be seen advancing, in line after line, the ends of which continued off to the horizon. The low-hanging sky displayed a faint brightness where it met the horizon, and the heroic figure in his ash-gray cloak and Napoleon hat was thrown into relief against the cold, cold sky. It was a scene to fill one with mournful thoughts.

"This picture—" Katsuko started explaining, without waiting for Copper's reply. "In 1814, Napoleon was marching to engage the allied forces of European nations that had invaded France. Now Napoleon's most powerful days were over. When he failed in his attack on Russia, countries throughout Europe rose together, rebelling against Napoleon, and eventually they invaded France. After Napoleon was defeated at the Battle of Leipzig, he returned to France, still fighting here and there with a ferocity that you could hardly call human. But when he caught wind of rumors that the European allies were going to invade France, Napoleon roused himself one more time, gathered his surviving forces, and went to beat them back.

"His soldiers were tired, their ammunition was low, the enemy army was several times larger than his, and even Napoleon, this time, couldn't say with confidence that he'd surely win. But still he set out. He resigned himself to a desperate fight and set out. To fight one final battle and reclaim his destiny.

"How do you think Napoleon felt at this time?"

"You mean, Napoleon won?" Copper asked.

"No, in the end he lost. And then he was captured and exiled to the isle of Elba. That's why, when I look at this picture, my heart becomes full. An inescapable, unhappy fate awaited him, but Napoleon had no choice but to fight toward it. Even if it meant he'd be thrown down by the enemy, he could never surrender and bow down to them. When I think about that and look at this picture, I have an indescribable feeling."

Copper, too, hearing that, felt largely the same about Napoleon's fate and thought it was somehow a tragic story. Kitami as well, receiving the postcard from Copper, gazed at it for quite a while with deep emotion. Uragawa, too, peered eagerly over from the side.

"Allons enfants de la Patrie . . ."

Katsuko, in a low voice, started to sing France's national anthem, "La Marseillaise."

Not long afterward, the four boys and Katsuko went out to the lawn, all warm from the sunlight, and were happily playing. Mizutani preferred art and music, and was not particularly good at sports, but Katsuko was a natural athlete, and she excelled at everything athletic. She was on the basketball and volleyball teams, in track she anchored the mixed sprint relay, and she held the record for high jump and long jump. Her favorites were the jumps, and actually, she was nursing hopes to join the Japanese women's track team in the next Olympics. Because of that, their father had installed an official jumping arena for Katsuko at the edge of the lawn, with a top-notch runway attached. The whitewashed measurement rod with the meters marked off was the real thing, and the high-jump bar was regulation as well, so it was exactly the same as the arena at Tokyo's Jingu Stadium and was a terrific thing. After Copper and his friends played catch, they did the triple jump and the long jump and the high jump, with Katsuko as instructor and coach.

When all was said and done, Copper and Kitami couldn't hold their own against Katsuko. Copper tried with all his might and finally made it over the one-meter bar, but immediately Katsuko, still with both hands jammed in her pockets, cleared it with ease. They gradually raised the bar, and in the end, Katsuko was the only survivor. There was nothing for Copper and company to do but watch Katsuko's good form as she jumped. In her yellow sweater and dark-blue pants, flipping over the bar and landing again on her feet, she was a wondrous figure.

When it came to the triple jump, Kitami showed terrific enthusiasm, saying "All right, now you'll see a jump with some heroic spirit!" but of course, he was no match for Katsuko. Uragawa, too, just for today, was not even a little embarrassed by his utter lack of ability and jumped again and again. In the triple jump, you start by leaping as far as you can, and then you do a quick one-foot hop for the second jump, and at first Uragawa couldn't do it at all. Katsuko coached him, patiently showing him any number of times how to do it. In the end, when Uragawa was finally able to do a proper jump, Copper, Kitami, Mizutani, and Katsuko all let out a huge cheer as if he had just set a new Olympic record.

Uragawa turned bright red but then beamed, unable to contain his happiness.

After they had played all the usual games, Uragawa suggested they try pole-pushing, a game in which each player took one end of a long stick and tried to push the other player back without letting go.

"I almost never lose that!" he blurted.

Mizutani quickly found a suitable bamboo stick. Copper went first and was easily pushed out of bounds by Uragawa.

Next was Mizutani's turn, but slipping and sliding, he was no match for their friend either. Kitami said, "Good. Now I'll have my revenge!" He spit on his hands and stepped up, but Uragawa was undaunted. Kitami planted his legs and pushed and heaved with so much effort that his face turned red, but eventually he was pushed back.

"What . . . what the . . ."

At this, Kitami redoubled his efforts and pushed for dear life, but slipping centimeter by centimeter, he was forced back, and finally, saying "What . . . what the . . ." all the way, he was defeated.

"Okay, one more time!" Copper again leaped into the fray, to no avail. Mizutani and Kitami took turn after turn, but no matter how many times they tried, it was no contest.

"You're too strong!" Kitami said in admiration, finally throwing in the towel.

"How can you be so strong?"

"How, you say?" Uragawa replied, laughing. "Well, sometimes in the evening I play with the store workers and use the shop's carrying pole, you see? So I have the knack."

The four of them had lunch in the dining room of the main house, together with Mizutani's mother and his older brother. From the high ceiling hung a grand decorative chandelier, and on the dark golden walls hung a large oil painting. On the dining table was a magnificent arrangement of fresh-cut greenhouse flowers in bloom, and the tablecloth was pure white. On top of that were fancy knives and forks and silver spoons—today's meal was a proper one. But even though Copper and his friends felt that they were treated with ceremony, somehow they couldn't tell whether the treat was delicious or not.

First, Mizutani's mother welcomed them kindly, but she seemed so thoroughly elegant, like some sort of princess, that they forgot themselves and couldn't reply. The older brother, too, sat next to Copper and his friends, but whether he saw them or not, from start to finish he just sat there primly and didn't utter a single word. Since he was wearing a Western-style suit, Kitami asked Mizutani "Your older brother, is he working somewhere?" but according to Mizutani's reply, it seemed he was still a university student and was studying philosophy. Perhaps when one studied philosophy, one became disinclined to speak with junior high school students.

It was a special occasion, but when lunch was over, Copper and his friends couldn't help but feel a little bit relieved. They hustled back to Mizutani and Katsuko's annex. At once they felt better and set about playing crokinole, Ping-Pong, cards, and all sorts of indoor games. Mizutani had enough of them to open a small store.

"You have it good—you have so many things to play with," Copper said without thinking.

"No, it's bad! I have nobody to play them with."

"Don't you have your sister?"

"Not really. Since my sister started high school, she doesn't play with me anymore."

"Doesn't your father play with you after he comes home from work?"

"Our dad has lots of meetings in the evening, and he's really busy. So usually I'm asleep when he comes home. Sometimes I don't see him for four or five days in a row!"

"Wow . . ."

"Also, my mother goes out a lot. So when I'm here alone, I listen to a record or paint a picture."

Copper thought that for Mizutani to live in a nice house like this one, and in a situation where everything he wanted was bought for him, and despite that for his everyday life to be so lonely, was a really strange thing.

"Well, you should come play at my house more often."

"For sure, I'd like that, too, but your mother might not like me to come so often."

"Don't worry about that!"

"Okay. My sister doesn't listen to what my mother says at all these days either—she just mostly does what she wants. My mother is a little weird. Like she asks me why I'm not friends with Hori and Haneda. As if I would play with selfish blabbermouths like them."

"Really. Those jerks! But why does your mom want you to be friends with them?"

"I wasn't sure why. But then my sister told me it's probably because Hori's father is a famous government official. And then Haneda's grandfather is a member of the House of Peers."

Copper whistled, impressed. "Official fathers, member grandfathers—I don't like those types. Don't they all follow Yamaguchi?"

"That's true. They all fawn on him. And they bad-mouth Kitami. I won't be friends with them. Even if it would suit my mother—"

Kitami must have overheard some of the conversation between Copper and Mizutani. He spoke as if he had just remembered something.

"That's right . . . about Yamaguchi . . . At the end of last term, I heard something strange!"

Everyone looked in Kitami's direction. He continued.

"The older students in the judo club said that Yamaguchi and I were going to get it sometime."

"You and Yamaguchi, you said?" Copper asked, surprised. No one had expected this, and they gathered around Kitami, but he replied with a calm face.

"Yeah, they said they were going to beat us up. I heard it from Higuchi in the second-year class."

In Copper's school, a movement had occurred recently to raise school spirit, centered around the older students in the judo club. According to this group, student morale in general had collapsed in recent days, a slipshod attitude had pervaded the school, and it would never do. They adopted the following principles:

First, that school spirit was severely lacking, and the cheering at sport competitions was not at all enthusiastic.

Second, that the younger students had become generally impudent, and they lacked respectful manners toward older students.

Third, that the number of people who had abandoned themselves to reading novels, seeing plays, or going to movies or musical revues had gradually increased. If things were to continue this way, the spirit of strength and resilience that had been the pride of the school since its founding would probably collapse. Thus, it was necessary to alert all the students in the school that they must reform their attitudes.

The group preached their dogma endlessly. There were also some who gave angry speeches at school assemblies, denouncing the state of affairs. And not just that—there were those who began to advocate punishing anyone who failed to show the proper school spirit.

"Make no mistake," they insisted, "once they enter society, students with no love of school will surely become citizens with no love of country. People who don't love their country are traitors. Therefore, we can say that students who don't love their school are traitors in training. We must discipline any such fledgling traitors."

Of course, it's right that students should love their own schools. We should love our schools and do our best to improve them, even just a little. Furthermore, younger students should have respect for their older, senior students, and as long as one is a student, it's best not to squander one's time with idle entertainment. If that were the end of it, there would be nothing wrong with what these senior judo-club students were claiming.

However, while they believed that their claims were correct, they had made up their minds that their judgments were also correct, each and every one. And then they assumed that people who rubbed them the wrong way were all in the wrong and rebelling against school spirit.

But the greatest arrogance of these people was to think that they were allowed to scold and punish other students for their failings. Who would expect their fellow students to do that?

But this group believed they could.

And so even though they believed they were acting to improve the school, they actually stirred up all sorts of trouble that had nothing to do with improving the school. They would say a student hadn't cheered adequately at a sporting event with another school, brand him a traitor or even worse, and beat him up. And because of their violent swaggering, even though they claimed to love their school, weren't they inadvertently making it into a place that was hard even to like?

Popular songs were forbidden, they said, and they couldn't stand to listen to endless poetry recitations either. But on top of that, the most important rule was that the little students of the lower school should tiptoe around in fear.

Since around the end of the second term, the first- and second-year students had been completely unable to relax. In the morning, there were those who forgot to bow when they met the older students on the road, and they would be summoned and forced to grovel. If someone wore a flashy wristwatch, they'd quickly get a sharp look, and then when the older students' gossip about them leaked out, they would get a reputation for having a bad attitude.

A student named Higuchi, in the second-year class, liked literature. He always had his nose buried in novels that grown-ups were reading, and went to see the latest plays, and so he was blacklisted. In the first-year group, Yamaguchi was a bit of a sharp dresser, and on top of that, he was a cinephile and had a collection of two hundred or more photos of movie actors, so he also attracted dirty looks.

"Gatchin" Kitami, stubborn as always, stuck to his own positions without budging, whether his opponent was older or not, so even though he was little, he was pegged as having a bad attitude.

And then, early in the third term, a rumor came up from somewhere that they had decided to levy sanctions on the blacklisted students.

When Higuchi heard the rumors about the punishments, he quietly informed Kitami, who was among the students who had fallen under similar condemnation.

"But leaving Yamaguchi aside, there's no reason to attack you, is there? You haven't done anything wrong—" Copper said heatedly.

"Well, at least two times when I met Kurokawa, I didn't make an effort to bow to him," Kitami responded. "And then, when we were fighting over who could use the sponge-ball court during recess one time, I didn't listen to what he said. Because I was definitely there first. So Kurokawa probably thinks I have a bad attitude."

Kurokawa was a fifth-year student, second-in-command on the judo team, and was as big as a grown-up, bigger even than the physical education teacher.

"Oh no! Him?"

Kitami continued angrily.

"Even though he's always saying that singing pop songs is disgraceful, he sings them himself! With a big, hoarse voice! I heard him on the steam train coming back from the last school trip. His song was a samurai song, so it's fine, he said. That's such a lame excuse! And when I heard his lousy voice, I hated him even more."

"But it's not worth getting beat up over, is it?"

"It'll be okay. If I don't do anything, Kurokawa won't attack me. He's just waiting to jump me if I do something. So I think I just have to be careful of that."

Maybe that's all there is to it, Copper thought uneasily.

Mizutani also looked worried and said, "But maybe they'll summon all the people they've been watching one by one and beat them up! I think you should tell the teacher about it."

"That's no good. If I do that, then they'll be even angrier. Then when they find a good excuse, they'll really hurt me. I think it's better just to take it easy."

"No way, that's dangerous!"

"Uh-uh, it'll be okay."

While Copper and Kitami were arguing, Katsuko came in carrying a dish of candies.

"You're all looking awfully serious. What are you going on about?"

Copper and Mizutani explained the dangerous situation Kitami was facing. When she heard the story, Katsuko was indignant.

"Really, such tyranny! Kitami, you absolutely mustn't give in. The school isn't there just for the older students. Obviously, first-year students are students as well, aren't they? If you follow the rules, if you do what the teacher says, even a first-year student should be allowed to hold his head high. I think there's no need to bow down before those jujitsu guys."

"But—it's dangerous for Kitami!" Mizutani interjected.

"Even if it's dangerous! If they see that they can make you crawl, doesn't that make thugs like that all the more swellheaded? Picking fights for the sake of the school—that's wrong! If they are really thinking about what's good for the school, everyone should be able to live their lives there happily, whether they are first-year students or who-ever. Those guys want to think they're the only defenders of justice. It's conceited! Kitami, it's wrong to bow down in spite of that!"

"That's right! No matter what anyone says, I won't surrender!" Kitami's "no matter what anyone says" had to come out eventually, but this time, Copper didn't take any pleasure in it. Thinking about what might happen if Kitami were actually beaten up, he was very worried. Even if it was good not to give in to the bullies, what in the world could they do to protect Kitami from danger?

Everyone had their own advice about this. Mizutani and Copper were of the opinion that it was best to tell the teacher right away and let the teacher handle it. Kitami felt that to do so might make things even harder for him, so he was of the opinion that he should do nothing. Katsuko thought that they should keep an eye on things for a little longer in any case and, when push came to shove, ask the teacher's advice and respond accordingly. However, there was a question as to whether they would know when was the right time to do that. In any case, Kitami himself would not agree to hurry off to the teacher now.

"You can say they're going to beat me—that's fine! I didn't do anything bad. I'm not going to get scared or anything just from listening to rumors. I don't like that."

Once Kitami had said that, there was little any of the others could do. Then Uragawa, who had been silent up until now, opened his mouth for the first time.

"Uh, I was thinking about what I'd do if I were in this situation, but—"

As one, everyone looked in Uragawa's direction, and Uragawa, a little bashfully, spoke.

"If Kitami gets called up by the older boys, well, we could all go together with him."

"And then what?" Copper asked.

"If it looks like Kurokawa and all of them are going to attack Kitami, we could say they have to attack all of us, too. We could tell them, if you're going to beat up Kitami, who didn't do anything, then you should beat us all up together. If we do that, then there's no way they'd beat us up!"

Everyone became silent.

"And then what if they say they're going to beat you up, too?" Katsuko asked.

"In that case . . . In that case, we all get beat up, together with Kitami. There will be nothing we can do about it."

"So great!!! Master Uragawa!" Katsuko leaped out of her chair. "That's it. That's best. Everyone must protect Kitami, and if that fails, then there's nothing to be done. Everyone meets the same fate as Kitami. That's the heroic spirit! When the time comes, I, too, shall support you. I'll have our father come to your school and negotiate for you. If father won't come, then mother, and if it seems like mother won't go, then I'll go myself. Then we'll speak to the headmaster and we'll have the judo club ejected from the school. So, Kitami, be strong! Hayao, you too must be strong with him!"

"I will." Mizutani tightened his lips with resolve and nodded his slender face resolutely.

"Copper, you too."

Copper nodded.

Kitami repeatedly tried to decline, saying that it was bad for everyone to meet the same fate for his sake, but everyone insisted that it was good and they weren't worried about that.

"Well, now that's decided—it's a shame I don't go to the same school as you, but if it comes to it, I will keep my promise to you. So shall we pinky-swear?"

Thereupon the four boys and Katsuko took a solemn, mutual, pinky-sworn oath.

The short winter day was drawing to an end.

Copper, Kitami, and Uragawa had to return home before the sun went down. The maid brought them three white cotton bundles, saying, "Please take these home with you." Inside each bundle was a box of marvelous sweets and a perfect apple.

Katsuko said, "Uragawa, you have a sister and brother, don't you? Here, please give these to them."

She stuffed his pockets with candies wrapped in pretty silver paper.

The three boys, each dangling his bundled souvenir of the visit, left Mizutani's house. Mizutani and Katsuko saw them off through the neighborhood. Katsuko rode a bicycle, slowly pushing the pedals, now nearer, now farther from the group of boys.

They came as far as the hill overlooking the Shinagawa sea, and Katsuko lightly dismounted from her bicycle. Everyone stopped for a moment to say their goodbyes.

As Copper and his friends, now three, descended the slope, a hazy dusk had fallen on the streets below them, and here and there glowing electric lights began to wink on. The train could be seen running along its track, as if it were gliding on ice. Trams and automobiles crossed busily at the foot of the slope. The commotion came floating up from the evening haze.

The three boys suddenly felt something akin to home-sickness and hurried off toward Shinagawa Station.

UNCLE'S NOTEBOOK

What Makes a Great Person:
On the Life of Napoleon

~~~~~~

Copper,

I was surprised to hear you had suddenly become a disciple of Napoleon, but after listening to your story, it seems this was due to the influence of Mizutani's sister, was it not?

Napoleon's life was certainly a magnificent one. If you measure his career in splendor or glory, people who compare are rare in the long history of humankind. There are young admirers of Napoleon everywhere, not just among you and your friends. His biography sells briskly all over the world.

Now, I know that at some point I have told you that when something makes a deep impression on you, you should remember it and reflect on its meaning later, right? So this evening, let's reflect, for one thing, on why Napoleon's life affected you in that way.

When we look at Napoleon's career, the first thing that strikes us is its remarkable level of activity.

Napoleon's father and mother were of fallen noble families on the island of Corsica, so he was raised in a state of some poverty. At exactly the age you are now, he had to leave his parents to enroll in military school in his home country of France. Among his fellow students there were many wealthy noble families. He was treated with contempt by his peers, became lonely, and kept to himself.

He left school and was commissioned to a regiment as a second lieutenant, then a full lieutenant, but even during that period, Napoleon was as poor as ever and unable to lead the carefree life of a young man. He was a pale and melancholy young officer who spent his days in study and avoided showy gatherings.

However, at the age of twenty-four, during the great upheaval of the French Revolution, this poor, scruffy officer became a brigadier general in a single leap. When the Republican army laid siege to the fort at Toulon, this young officer performed great works, distinguishing himself.

And what happened after that, you already know—the famous crossing of the Alps. Leading a ragged army that was as poorly trained as it was ill equipped, he made his surprise crossing of the Alps, rolled down across the Italian plains like an avalanche, crushed the great Austrian army in a flash, and moving on, sacked the cities and towns of Italy, one after the next.

Wherever he went—victory, victory, victory.

When he returned to Paris with all his spoils of war, he had already become a great, triumphant general and the center of popularity in Paris.

At that time, in the wake of the great revolution in France, political conflict became more severe each year, and there seemed no end of fear and anxiety. The French people were starting to want nothing more than peace and order in the country. Seizing the moment, Napoleon orchestrated a military coup of the government, and step by step, he consolidated power in his own hands.

First he became one of three consuls, then he became a permanent, lifelong consul, and at last he abandoned the French Republic and assumed for himself the title of emperor.

Copper! Think of how old Napoleon was at this time. He was thirty-five. In a scant ten years, he had made a lightning ascent in a single breath, from the circumstances of a poor undistinguished officer whom nobody would look at twice, to the throne of the emperor. There's no success story as spectacular as this one.

Even after Napoleon became emperor, his star was still on the rise. The countries of Europe had formed an alliance centered around Great Britain, and they tried to topple him time and again, but all such efforts met with failure. Waging war after war, as if to demonstrate his genius as a soldier, Napoleon fought at Austerlitz, at Jena, at Wagram, and the longer he fought, the longer his string of historic victories continued.

Holland was among the first to yield, but now, as Napoleon built on his control of the Italian peninsula, Germany, too, succumbed to his might, and then Spain was forced to bow down as well. All at once, the whole of the European continent, with the exception of Russia in the east, had come to submit to his authority.

In 1808, when Napoleon held an all-Europe conference in Erfurt, four kings and thirty-four princes from Germany gathered to meet him. Surrounded by the royals, he attended a number of plays by the great actor Talma, who had been brought there expressly for this purpose. At this time, Napoleon was literally a king among kings.

In this way, Napoleon reached his heyday, during which the destiny of many tens of millions of people living in Europe came under the sway of just one man, to do with as he pleased. Napoleon had attained the pinnacle of his powers.

However, just a few short years after this pinnacle, he would fall helter-skelter to the depths of destruction. And the start of that downfall was—you also know this—the failure of his great campaign against Russia.

You may wonder why in the world Napoleon attacked Russia. This was because Russia was not following his orders and refused to stop trading with Great Britain. As an island nation, Great Britain had remained hostile to Napoleon from the first to the last, relying on the fact that it was separated from the European continent, and it refused to yield to his authority in the slightest. In order to weaken Great Britain, Napoleon finally prohibited all trade between it and the European continent, but this effort was doomed to failure from the start. So eventually Napoleon lost patience and planned a large-scale military campaign against Russia.

This, as you know, ended in disaster. In individual battles, he scored great victories and even managed to occupy the Russian capital, Moscow, but facing food shortages and bitter cold, with no decisive victory in sight, the great Napoleon was eventually forced to begin a retreat.

Suffering nearly to the point of starvation, marching through snow and ice, hundreds of thousands of soldiers froze to death during the retreat. Those who didn't die in vain of cold were killed by the pursuing Cossacks. And the army, which numbered more than six hundred thousand when it first invaded Russia, reached its home border with fewer than ten thousand men, terminating its campaign in a miserable state.

When news of this great loss reverberated around Europe, the first to rise and take up arms was Prussia, which had long tried to shake off Napoleon's oppression and was waiting for just this opportunity. After that, the other countries formed an alliance and rebelled against Napoleon all at once, attacking France from all sides.

And then even Napoleon had his moment of downfall. He couldn't hold off the allied forces. He was defeated in battle, captured, and exiled to the island of Elba.

He did escape once from Elba after that. He gathered his soldiers and tried for one last decisive victory at the famous Battle of Waterloo, but when this, too, ended in defeat, he was, in the end, confined like a prisoner on the isle of Saint Helena, far off the west coast of Africa.

For five and a half years on this tiny island, with its poor climate, Napoleon lived a life of hardship, and eventually he died a lonely death.

Now, at the time he lost that last decisive battle, Napoleon was forty-six years old. So he, who in a mere ten years had risen so quickly from destitute officer to emperor, had fallen again, in another ten years, from emperor to broken-bodied prisoner of war.

If you talk about Napoleon's remarkable career in terms of time gone by, you could say he crammed his entire life into those twenty years.

It was only twenty years, but those twenty years were certainly magnificent. During that time, one poor but brilliant officer rose to the status of all the rulers of Europe combined, and then tumbled again from that throne. It tugs at the heart like a fairy tale, but there's more. The degree of activity Napoleon displayed during this twenty-year period is so nearly inhuman that it's astounding.

Running from the end of the eighteenth century to the beginning of the nineteenth, and starting with the French Revolution, these twenty years marked a period of nonstop, seething upheaval in the European landscape. Problems arose one after another, and it was a period so rich in events that it was the equal of fifty or even a hundred years in any other era. And it's fair to say that each historic event that happened during this time was connected to the name of Napoleon.

Copper, I don't know if you know this or not, but here in Japan, they say that most of our prime ministers develop physical ailments after serving for two or three years. So working as prime minister can damage your health, and some think it may actually shorten your life span. Even being the prime minister of a single country, during peacetime, without having to make history, is so demanding that it drains your life force away, just like that. Think that over, then look at Napoleon's career.

He had to hammer together a new order in France after its great upheaval. He had to fight off foreign invasions constantly. And on top of all that, without a moment of rest, he had to weather the rough seas of diplomatic relations from his position at the very center of European politics. He undertook this work in majestic form, resolving both domestic issues and foreign affairs all on his own, but that wasn't all. At the same time, he fought three or four wars like nothing before in history, one after another, and each time he commanded a great army, while he himself stood on the battlefield in person. Is that not a truly astounding spirit?

And it's not only that he took this work upon himself and dug into it and bore up under it. When it comes to warfare, Napoleon's campaigns, aside from the failure of the one in Russia, were some of the most marvelous of all time. To this day, military tacticians use them as models. Even off the field of battle, his decisions were bold, his actions were positive, and he never hesitated in the slightest. He stretched himself to the breaking point as if he didn't know the meaning of exhaustion, and no matter what difficulties he encountered, he faced them with courage and pride worthy of a king. No one could help but marvel at a man who was this strong and had such vigor. Even the great German writer Goethe, who loved peace and humanity, and who nursed great hopes for the advancement of the human race, admired Napoleon's boundless vitality and force of will with all his heart and was moved to tell of this.

Yes, Napoleon certainly embodied greatness. He was a hero worthy of the name. During the early years in which he raced to the pinnacle of power, pulling himself up from adversity by his bootstraps, he was so youthful, so brilliant, so energetic that just to read his biography is to have your eyes opened wider. And when it came to his golden days, when he reigned over all Europe as one of the great monarchs of world history, he was every bit as magnificent as the sun. His downfall, too, was also a great tragic drama. It's not at all unreasonable that you or your friends might worship him or that even people like Goethe would admire him.

And yet—

And yet, Copper, when we say that we admire Napoleon's career because of its remarkable vitality, there's one point that we must not forget.

Of course, when we wonder how it's possible for a human being to accomplish such a remarkable amount in his life, we can't help but be surprised. No, not only surprised. When it comes to human beings, there are certain things you can rely on. It's the reason that we feel good when we read Napoleon's biography, and why Napoleon's biography is still read with love. But whether we call it accomplishment, vitality, or spirit, what in the world is it? Isn't it the power to achieve something? The power to realize some purpose in the world?

If so, then we can admire Napoleon's great vitality, and while we do, we can also ask the question, "What in the world did Napoleon, with this wonderful vitality, accomplish?"

Copper, this is not just about Napoleon. You must ask questions like this of any great person or hero.

The people that we call great or heroic are all of them extraordinary people. They have abilities that everyday people do not, and can accomplish things that everyday people can't. Being extraordinary means that they all have something about them to make us bow down.

But more than humbling ourselves to these people, we must be bold enough to ask questions. Such as "What did they accomplish using these extraordinary abilities?" Or "Of what use are their extraordinary accomplishments?"

And with extraordinary abilities, isn't it possible that one might just as easily accomplish extraordinarily bad things?

Copper, when you ask such a question, it's essential that you bear one thing in mind. You must consider the tens of thousands of years of the long, long history of progress of the human race. Because no matter who the so-called hero is—whether it's Napoleon or Goethe or even Toyotomi Hideyoshi, who ruled all of Japan in the sixteenth century, or General Nogi, who commanded the Japanese army during the war against Russia—all of them were born during this long, long march of human history and will die within it as well.

As you know well by now, people built our world only by working together, and through that mutual effort we escaped from our primitive state. Using very simple tools at first and eventually discovering all sorts of technology and machines, step by step we changed the natural world into a better place for people to live. And along with that, we created art and science and gradually changed human life into a bright and beautiful thing.

These changes have flowed slowly and steadily down from the distant past and continue to flow onward from here, away again, like a great river.

We say that the history of Japan starts with Emperor Jimmu, two thousand six hundred years ago, and that the civilization of Egypt began more than six thousand years ago, and we think of those as terribly old things, but actually, there's a history of many tens of thousands of years before that, when nothing could be written. And from this moment on, won't the human race probably continue to progress for many tens of thousands or even hundreds of thousands of years?

Consider this tremendous current, flowing so slowly and endlessly. Doesn't two thousand or even three thousand years' time come to seem short? And doesn't a single human life seem no longer than the blink of an eye?

Copper! Cast your inner eye once over this vast landscape, look back at the people called great and heroic in the midst of that faraway flow, and what kinds of things might you come to see?

First, you might notice that the great people and heroes that loomed so large in your eyes until now were, ultimately, no more than drops of water drifting in that great stream.

Next, you'd surely see that no matter what things those extraordinary people did, they were exceptionally fleeting, unless their work was firmly bound to the current of the stream.

Some among them, watching this stream, pour the whole of their brief lives into it, devoting their extraordinary abilities to driving it forward properly.

Still others, in an effort to further their own individual goals, are completely unaware that they are helping the stream to advance.

And then there are those in the stream who, however much they may surprise the world with their brilliance, are not of the slightest use to the great current. No, there are more than a few who may be called great or heroic, but instead of advancing the flow, they work instead to try to reverse it.

And finally, there are times when one hero will do many things, some with the current and others against. In the course of history, many people arise and do many different things, but ultimately, if what they do is not consistent with the flow of that current, all the accomplishments of any one person will, finally and fleetingly, fall to ruin.

So, Copper, even such a man as Napoleon can't escape being an example of this. Now let's look at him one more time.

When Napoleon was taking his first steps toward success, the French people overthrew their corrupt feudal system in a bloody effort to build a new society. But at that time, other

European nations were still clinging to feudalism, so they feared this new nation in France and sent their armies, working together to try to defeat this new French government.

France was suffering terribly as a result of civil war and foreign invasion, both at the same time. But in the midst of these troubles, the French people fought bravely and never let themselves be beaten down. They required military service for all men, quickly organized an army, and mustered a force of eighty thousand to strike at the foreign invaders.

At that time, European countries generally used what was called a mercenary system to make up their armies. Soldiers received a salary and fought in return for their pay. On the other hand, the soldiers making up the French army were the newly freed masses of the French population, fighting on behalf of their new government.

They were people who were glad to lay down their own lives for the sake of their beloved homeland. Under the banner of "freedom, equality, fraternity," the French people, who had just given birth to a new era, were filled with an energy and a courage that the hired soldiers couldn't even imagine.

So although they were poorly trained and short of weapons and ammunition, the French soldiers faced the invaders with remarkable spirit and eventually drove them off, defending their homeland. And at the head of this new army, with strategies designed specifically for it, was none other than

Napoleon, mowing down the old-fashioned armies of Europe, one after the next.

So at least until he became emperor, Napoleon was certainly useful, wasn't he? He helped to protect France, which was trying to overthrow the feudal system and create a new free society.

And not just that. He made great efforts to encourage the arts and sciences. You may already know this from reading "The Mysterious History of Writing" in your book *Mysteries of the World*, but at the time of his Egyptian expedition, he enlisted many scholars and artists to travel with his army and had them engage in research on Egypt. You may understand, too, how useful this was to the later development of the field of Egyptology. The stela called the Rosetta stone, which was discovered at this time, became an important key to deciphering Egyptian hieroglyphics.

Later, when the French people tired of civil war and cried out for domestic peace and order, Napoleon took advantage of this to consolidate power, but as long as his strength created order and stability for the new society, even this personally ambitious action was useful to the world. It made it clear what the new social order would be, after the eradication of the feudal system. He gathered scholars and had them set forth that new order clearly in laws. This was the famous Napoleonic Code. It became a model for the laws of countries all over, and one could perhaps say that this was the greatest of Napoleon's accomplishments.

This may surprise you, but even here in Japan we owe a lot to this legal code.

During the Meiji Restoration in the nineteenth century, Japan also abolished feudalism and turned to a society of equality for people of all classes. At that point, how best to determine relations between people in this new social order quickly become a problem. So the first civil laws were established, and at that time they used the Napoleonic Code as an example.

There have been various amendments to our civil code since then, but its foundation remains unchanged. And advancing along these lines, new Japan has achieved remarkable commercial and industrial progress since its beginnings.

In this way, Napoleon was useful to the world. He helped introduce the new era that would replace the feudal era, and then he took advantage of this progress to reap one brilliant success after another. But in due course, as he became emperor, he turned to the exercise of power for its own sake. And trying to strengthen his own influence without bounds, he in turn lost the gratitude of many people in society.

His greatest failure was to forbid all continental-European trade with Great Britain, in an attempt to bring suffering to the nation that had so doggedly resisted him.

Napoleon believed that he could do whatever he had the power to do. And what's more, he thought that he had to do those things in order to maintain his power.

However, when he tried to ban all trade with Great Britain, his plan backfired. At the time, Britain controlled sea trade throughout the world, so instead of creating problems for Great Britain, his plan created problems for the tens of millions of people who lived on the European continent. People at that time fell short even on items like sugar, which they used every day. In Europe, no matter how many sugar beets they tried to grow, they couldn't make enough sugar to satisfy the needs of the population. And no matter how Napoleon strengthened his influence, he couldn't stifle the living needs of so many people.

He enforced his ban by laying down strict penalties, but no matter what he did, his commands weren't obeyed. Despite great effort, his policy ended in failure, and on top of that, he earned the resentment of those millions of people.

The failure of the Russia campaign had its origins there. Six hundred thousand people set out for faraway Russia, and when you stop to think that nearly all of them died miserably, in ice and snow, that was really quite a major event.

These people were soldiers assembled from lands all over Europe, and when they set out for Russia, they weren't fighting for their own countries. They weren't fighting for the honor of their homelands, nor were they fighting for their faith or prin-ciples. They were laying down their lives to protect nothing at all, dragged off to Russia on Napoleon's power to die meaning-lessly, a sacrifice to his ambition.

Six hundred thousand people! And as surely as each of them had a family, you can be certain they had friends as well, who also loved them. So the result wasn't just the death of six hundred thousand people; millions of living people also plunged into utter despair, crying bitter tears.

Once it came to this—yes, to the point where he became a person who had caused so much suffering to so many people—Napoleon's authority had already transformed into something harmful to the proper advancement of society. His downfall was already inevitable.

And in fact, history proved that to be true.

Copper, if we just examine Napoleon's life thus far, we can already see it clearly. Among those we call heroic and great, the only people we can truly respect are those who have helped to advance the human race. And among all the achievements of these people, only the ones that follow the flow of this advanc-ing current have true value.

If you have the time, please try reading a book called *Great Benefactors of Mankind*. You will most likely see that among the so-called greats there is a completely different type of person.

And then, by and by, when you have a solid understanding of this, you will have to take a fresh look at Napoleon and put some effort into learning what can be learned from him.

His hard-fought life, his courage, his determination, and then his iron will!

Because without these, even if one wanted to advance humanity, one wouldn't be able to bear up under the strain. You must delve ever so deeply into the resolute spirit of the man who faced such hardship without uttering a word of surrender, who met his hard fate undaunted.

Perhaps you know this story about Napoleon:

Routed at Waterloo, Napoleon was no longer safe anywhere in Europe. He attempted to cross to America from the port of Rochefort, but by that time this port had been occupied by the British, and he was at last taken prisoner.

The British navy immediately bore him back to its home country. While the steamer that was carrying Napoleon, called *Bellerophon*, was anchored at the mouth of the river Thames, the wharves were thronged daily with great numbers of sightseers.

You see, it's not unreasonable that the British people would rejoice that Napoleon, the fearsome and invincible hero who had raised such a tempest throughout Europe these past twenty years, should at last be taken prisoner and carried there.

After all, Napoleon was the opponent they had been fighting from start to finish and at whose hands they had tasted bitter defeat more than once. And now he was captured at last and brought to their own country. The crowds wanted at least to catch a glimpse of the boat that carried him.

Since he had arrived in Great Britain, Napoleon had been confined to his cabin, so although the people gathered along the wharves were hoping to catch a glimpse of him, they were unable to do so. But one day, Napoleon at last wanted to feel the touch of fresh air and appeared on the deck of the ship.

When they recognized the unexpected figure atop the deck of HMS *Bellerophon*, wearing the famous Napoleon hat, tens of thousands of onlookers involuntarily gasped. The wharves, which had been clamoring up to that moment, fell at once into a hush. And then, the next instant—Copper, what do you think happened? Tens of thousands of British people removed their hats without a word and silently stood, in a display of deep respect.

Defeated in battle, unwelcome in Europe, now captive in the hands of his nemesis of many years and borne back to its homeland, Napoleon didn't reveal himself to be a pitiful, dispirited figure. Even as a captive he stood firmly, with the pride of a king, bravely ready to face a fate of his own making.

And that spirited demeanor touched the hearts of tens of thousands of people and caused them to bow their heads. What strength of character the man must have had!

When you, too, become an adult, you will eventually come to know how many small, virtuous people there are who have the best intentions but who cannot realize them, all because of weakness.

The world is full of people who are not bad, but weak, people who bring unnecessary misfortune upon themselves and others for no reason but weakness. A heroic spirit that's not devoted to human progress may be empty and meaningless, but goodness that is lacking in the spirit of heroism is often empty as well.

I think that you too, now, will surely have a thing or two to consider.

Chapter Six

Events on a Snowy Day

Once the third term began, the rumors that Copper and his friends had heard spread like wildfire through the lower school. An uneasy feeling that something scary was about to happen haunted the thoughts of the smaller kids.

But a week passed, then two, and then somehow it was already February, and nothing particularly frightening had happened. School entrance exams were near at hand for the fourth- and fifth-year students, and busy with preparations for these, perhaps they could no longer be bothered about the younger students. It began to seem that the rumors were baseless and would disappear just like that.

But when Copper would come across four or five members of the judo club jostling noisily in the schoolyard, he felt a strange apprehension. When he saw them in the school corridors, especially, and had to meet their gazes somehow as he passed by, he couldn't express how bad he felt at those times.

From Copper's point of view, Kurokawa and his lot were towering giants. Kurokawa's face was thick skinned and pimply, like the rind of a bitter orange, and with his big grin he seemed at times to be laughing at Copper. When Copper saw that, a cold shiver would run down his spine.

In spite of that, Kitami, who was the subject of all this worry, didn't seem the least bit bothered. When he walked by the older boys, he held his head high, and if they swaggered like sailors on the docks, he would puff up his chest in return and strut by. Then, after he was safely past, he'd look back at the big group and with a careless air say something like, "Boy, what a bunch of gangsters!"

Copper, walking together with him, would always tremble, thinking about what could happen if they heard.

As for Yamaguchi, who was getting similar dirty looks from the older students, he was acting just like a mouse who had heard the cat meow. He'd sneak around, taking pains not to catch their attention, and even during recess, he played only with his closest friends, in the shadow of the kendo hall, which was some distance from the school-yard, or at the back of the gymnasium on rainy days.

Thanks to all of that, Uragawa was able to escape the persistent badgering of Yamaguchi and his crowd and enjoy some days of relative peace.

In this way the Emperor's Day holiday passed, and the remainder of February was dwindling, but as before, nothing much seemed to be happening. Even the cowardly Yamaguchi started to think that from here on, somehow, the coast would be clear.

But then one day, all because of a pointless little accident, Copper and his friends finally came face-to-face with the situation they had feared.

The light sleet that had started to fall the previous evening turned to full snow during the night, and when morning came, it showed no inclination to let up, continuing until around noon. At last, a snowy day!

The students were all wide-eyed with excitement at the long-awaited snowfall. The previous several days had been dark and bone cold, one after the next, and had left them numb to their very cores. But now the snow was here at last, and life returned to everyone's faces.

In the morning, while the snow was still falling, one could already see the figures of any number of students playing in the schoolyard, jumping cheerfully around in the snow.

Around noon the snow let up, and just when everyone was wondering whether the sky would clear, the sun burst through and began to shine. The yard during recess was so busy that it looked as if it were boiling. Everywhere you turned was pure white, glittering, and so dazzling you could hardly open your eyes.

In the midst of that, a jumble of students, one hundred or more, were moving in all directions. Chasing, being chased, slipping and sliding everywhere, joking and jostling as they passed each other, laughing voices colliding in the air.

Snowballs flew wildly in the sunlight. Children were dashing around, madly tossing armfuls of snow on each other like fountains. The next moment, the crowd parted unexpectedly, and a tremendous snowball appeared. Five or six children, working together, were rolling it along the ground. The bright air was buzzing with cheerful voices, exactly like a big beehive.

Of course, Copper was at the center of this maelstrom. Throwing snow, having snow thrown on him, wrestling and tumbling, romping around like a puppy dog. He was sweating all over, and his face was steaming in the cold air.

The forty-five-minute recess seemed way too short. When the bell rang for afternoon classes, everyone reluctantly retreated to the school building. The hundreds of students turned into a black river that was sucked into the school, leaving in its wake only the thoroughly trampled field of snow. And also, here and there in the yard, snowmen of various sizes and funny shapes were standing, having appeared during recess, each facing stubbornly in its own direction.

During the afternoon hours, Copper couldn't seem to focus on his studies. His heart was still thumping, the blood running warm in his body. Through the window, the sun-drenched snow outside glittered, and its reflection brightened the ceiling of the classroom.

One of the other classes seemed to have organized a snowball fight during gym period, and now and then he could hear loud, sharp battle cries. Copper's eyes kept wandering out through the window.

When the last class had finally ended, Copper jumped up like a spring that had slipped its catch. He dumped his books and notebook in his bag, flew down the corridor, and leaped out into the schoolyard.

While he quickly armed himself with three or four snowballs, Kitami and Mizutani came out, talking together about something or other. They were completely unaware that Copper was waiting for them. Copper laughed slyly to himself and silently let fly a shot at Kitami. Although the distance was considerable, the snowball miraculously scored a direct hit, right on the noggin.

Caught off guard, Kitami scanned the vicinity with an annoyed look on his face.

"Who did that?"

He continued to look this way and that for his unseen attacker, until Copper could stand it no longer and erupted in a yell: "Aaiiie!"

Kitami spotted Copper. His angry face immediately relaxed into a grin.

"Aha! It was you!!"

Already he had slipped his schoolbag from his shoulder and hung it on a hook on the school building.

"Let's go!"

Looking back at Mizutani as if to say, *That didn't take long*, Kitami immediately set about packing snow into ammunition. Mizutani, too, hurriedly hung up his bag and started making snowballs as fast as he could. When all was ready, they charged toward Copper, smiling, but with a fierce gleam in their eyes.

Copper held his ground, hurling a second and third snowball, but when he saw that they missed their marks, he spun quickly, turned tail, and fled. Three or four snowballs that came from behind blurred the air as they flew by him.

"After him!" Kitami shouted. Kitami and Mizutani darted in pursuit of Copper like a pair of foxhounds.

Copper fled cunningly, threading his way between the other students playing in the schoolyard. Then, hiding in the shade of a snowman, he hastily rearmed himself with snowballs, and when he spotted Kitami and company approaching, he fired two or three shots and again took off running.

Kitami got hit hard on the arm, and Mizutani took one on the chin. All the more excited, the two of them charged in hot pursuit of Copper, who took a solid shot himself that landed with a thud in the center of his back.

In this way, with Copper dodging, and Kitami and Mizutani in pursuit, the three of them running here and there and ducking between students, they gradually drifted to the far edge of the yard. Copper was in a frenzy. At some point, he had gotten the idea that he was Napoleon, the two boys chasing him were the allied armies of Austria and Russia, and the snowball fight was the Battle of Wagram.

Copper dug in at the end of the schoolyard, by a large snowman with one arm sticking out and a flowerpot for a hat, like a Turkish fez. Hidden behind this, Copper rained heavy fire upon the enemy for a while, but choosing his moment, he abandoned this encampment and searched for the next camp while he ran.

When he started to run, Kitami and Mizutani gave a loud shout and charged forward.

Copper still had two snowball bullets in his hands. After he had run a little bit, he thought *Okay, here's a good spot for a shot* and stopped in his tracks. He intended to engage the pursuing enemy. He spun around, but as he turned, he had a real shock. His pursuers had disappeared.

I wonder what happened to them? Copper thought. A little disappointed, he cast around for his targets. Instead, he saw a crowd gathering around the snowman where he had made his earlier stand. There were also students running toward the crowd, saying, "What is it? What's happening?" Copper, too, hurried back that way.

When Copper drew near, his heart nearly skipped a beat. Kitami and Mizutani were standing there, surrounded by five or six older students. And right in front of them was none other than Kurokawa from the judo club.

Kitami stood looking up at him, a grim expression on his face. Mizutani stood quietly next to Kitami, his eyes slightly downcast.

"Hey! Apologize, you! Apologize!" Kurokawa glared down at Kitami, arms crossed. "What do you think you're doing? We made this ourselves, with our own hands, and you have nothing to say for yourself? How dare you!"

"But I didn't know," Kitami quickly replied, head still held high.

"You didn't know? Liar!" Kurokawa growled and pointed at the snowman next to him. "Look! You do that, and then say you don't know. Who do you think you're talking to?"

The snowman with the flowerpot on its head was standing there as before, but now its one arm had been torn off, and the bare bamboo rod at its core was jutting out like a broken bone.

"I was just concentrating on running. I didn't break it on purpose. I didn't know," Kitami said, a little breathlessly.

"Shut your mouth!" Kurokawa roared in a frightening voice. "I don't need to hear excuses. Admit you're wrong and apologize! Apologize, now!"

For a while Kitami looked Kurokawa in the eye, but soon, in a low voice, he said, "I'll apologize."

"Well, if you apologize, we'll let it pass. Now apologize to all of us here!"

Kitami lowered his face and quietly said, "I'm sorry. Please forgive me."

Copper, who was watching, let out a sigh of relief. He had been worried, but somehow everything seemed to be turning out safely. But despite that, the next instant angry comments came flying pell-mell from the older students gathered round.

"I couldn't hear that!"

"Say it louder!"

"Speak clearly! Clearly!"

Kitami kept his head down and said nothing.

"Hey, you—speak up clearly!"

"Well, if he's going to talk in a whiny little mosquito voice . . ."

"Can't he speak?"

Enduring the barbs coming from all sides, Kitami stood silently. Next to Kurokawa, an older student, whose head was completely shaved on both sides, called out in irritation, "Well, can't you hear us? Speak up and apologize clearly. If you're going to apologize, then apologize right now—get to it!"

Kurokawa, too, puffed up his chest like a big shot.

"Kitami! You're going to apologize again so everyone can hear. That's the only way."

Kitami looked up again. He was deeply upset. His eyes flashed, and one corner of his mouth was twitching. For a while his lips trembled, but eventually he spoke as if he was spitting out the words: "Forgive me!" He spoke clearly, but his tone of voice was as sharp as a slap in the face. At once a murmur rose up from the older students.

"What? He talks like that?"

"That was an apology?"

"That's rude!"

As they were about to press forward in a mass, Kurokawa coolly held them back and stepped in front of Kitami.

"You, Kitami! That was a bit rude." Kurokawa's voice was unsettlingly calm. "What in the world must you think of us?"

" . . ."

"To you we are senior students. You're always rude to us, even though you're younger. It's always rude not to respect your elders—isn't that true? Until now we've been willing to overlook that, because it's your first year here, but if you take an attitude like this, we'll have to do something about it."

"That's right—we will!" someone called out.

At that, Kitami, with his lips pressed tight and a sullen expression on his face, said not a word. The students standing around watching the show looked back and forth between the two boys, from Kurokawa to Kitami in turn, wondering what would happen next.

Copper had no idea what to do. He stood there nervously, able neither to take his place with his friends nor to walk away. He could feel his pulse beating strong in his neck.

At that moment, Mizutani broke in.

"Kitami . . . Kitami didn't do it on purpose. It was a mistake. So—"

"You shut your mouth!" Kurokawa interrupted him forcefully, then spoke again.

"Kitami! What will it be? Will you do as we say from now on, and behave like a younger student should? Or will you disobey us? Answer! And then face the consequences."

As before, Kitami said not a word.

"Which is it? If you don't say, we can't know. Will you do as we say?"

"No," Kitami declared in a miserable voice. He closed his eyes and shook his head violently.

"What—?!" Pushing Kurokawa aside and moving in front of him was the shave-headed boy from before. Shavehead, looking like he had lost all patience, stepped up to Kitami. It seemed like he might strike Kitami at any moment, but just then, rushing in from out of nowhere, arms flailing—was none other than Uragawa.

Uragawa stopped in front of Shavehead.

"Kitami, he d–didn't do anything wrong! We . . . we . . ."

Uragawa was too worked up to say any more. Perhaps not knowing what to say, he flapped his hands over and over and tried desperately to speak but lapsed into a stammer.

"What do you want here, Tofu Boy?" Shavehead gave Uragawa a shove and sent him flying. Uragawa staggered back, reeling, then collapsed on his backside in the snow. Kurokawa's gang burst out laughing.

However, before the laughter had died down, there was a ghastly smack. Shavehead had slapped Kitami across the face, and his eyes had turned menacing.

"You . . . ! You think the school can maintain proper order with students like you?"

And he went after Kitami again, but instantly Mizutani wedged himself between them. Uragawa, too, after being dumped on his rear, had jumped up and run over to join them. The two of them stood together in Kitami's defense, pale faced and trembling, but nonetheless blocking the way.

This was the moment when he, too, could jump in, Copper thought.

But when he thought more about it, his whole body started to shake, and he found himself unable to run to them. *Now!* he thought. *Now is the time!* But somehow Copper just couldn't bring himself to act and instead just stood there.

"Hey, these guys are funny!" said Kurokawa, and his cheeks rose in an awful grin. "So you're sticking up for Kitami, are you? You're siding with him against us? Interesting. Well, give it your best shot, and let's see what happens."

Then Kurokawa took a long look at the younger students standing all around.

"Any other friends of Kitami here? Come on out!"

His voice was terrifying. Almost involuntarily, Copper lowered his head. His hands, still holding the snowballs, hid themselves of their own accord behind his back.

"Any more like these two? If so, get out here!" shouted Shavehead, following Kurokawa's lead and giving a hard, nasty look all around. Copper felt like those eyes had landed on him, and he shivered. Then he quietly and involuntarily dropped the snowballs hidden behind his back. He stood there, frozen, face lowered.

"Hey!" Copper could hear Mizutani shouting, and then he heard Kurokawa pass sentence. "Kitami! You will be punished!" After that, twice in succession, the dull thud of a fist on a body.

"Yes! Do it now!"

Kurokawa's group shouted with one voice. When Copper dared to look up, Kitami was sprawled at the foot of the snowman, and Uragawa and Mizutani were huddled together in front of him, in the midst of a barrage of snow bullets.

The snowballs came fast and hard, pummeling Mizutani and Uragawa in the face, in the chest, and even below the belt—everywhere, without discrimination. But the two of them stood staunchly together and didn't leave Kitami's side.

Clang! Clang! Clang!

The bell for class rang out from the school building. Copper and his friends had already been let out for the day, but the older students still had classes to attend. Hearing the sound of the bell, the judo club seniors took their parting shots, one by one, and withdrew from the field.

With the older students gone, Mizutani moved to Kitami's side and helped him get up. Uragawa picked up Kitami's fallen hat and placed it back on his head. Gritting his teeth, Kitami stood up, but suddenly he shouted, "Damn it!"

And without warning he flung himself at the body of the snowman. The snowman buckled at its midpoint, and its top half tumbled to the ground, where it smashed into bits of powdered snow. But Kitami took no notice of this and began to attack the remaining pieces of the body, even as Mizutani continued to hold him.

"It's not fair!" Kitami moaned between clenched teeth, and at this it seemed that the tears he had been holding back for so long could no longer be restrained. He sank his face into Mizutani's shoulder and cried until his body shook.

Tears quickly welled up in Mizutani's eyes as well.

The two of them stood there, arms around each other, and sobbed.

Uragawa cried, too, as if he couldn't bear it any longer, covering his face with the backs of his dirty hands until they were wet with tears.

After Kurokawa and the other older students had withdrawn, the classmates and second- and third-year friends of the three boys gathered round them, but seeing the situation and not knowing what to say, they drifted away in twos and threes, whispering among themselves, until the crowd had dissipated.

And then just the three tearful boys remained—and Copper.

Copper stood there dejectedly, head hanging down. His face was pale, and he gazed emptily at his feet without moving.

The sun continued to throw its bright light down from above the school building on the other side of the schoolyard, but nothing could have been lonelier than Copper's figure, casting its long shadow across the yard.

Yes, Copper had fallen into a dark, dark world.

Although he tried not to listen, he could hear a silent voice.

Coward.

    Coward.

      Coward.

Copper had broken the solemn promise he had made at Mizutani's house on the fifth day of the new year: that if they were attacked, they would all stick together. He had watched his good friend Kitami get attacked, and without a word of protest, without doing anything at all to save him, he had lamely watched the whole thing happen.

While on the other hand, Mizutani and Uragawa had kept the promise perfectly and together stepped up to share Kitami's fate.

Copper couldn't lift his head. Now, a mere five or six meters away, Kitami and his other friends were crying and consoling each other, but he couldn't bring himself to go to them or even to call out.

Just a short while ago, these had been his closest friends in the world. Now it seemed that they were receding into the distance, like strangers to him already, and might never be friends with him again. It felt like he had fallen into a deep, dark ravine, abandoned alone at the bottom of an unscalable cliff.

What had he done? What a foolish thing that could never be taken back!

Copper himself didn't understand how he could have done anything like this.

Downcast, he played over the events of those brief fifteen or sixteen minutes in his head. They reminded him of a bad dream. The figure of Kitami, surrounded by the older boys, standing firm, face held high. Kurokawa's profile, the spiteful look of the boy with the shaved head. And then Mizutani's intense, earnest expression as he stood at Kitami's defense, and Uragawa, trying with all his might to speak, looking all the while like he was going to burst into tears . . .

Yes, it would have been better by far, Copper thought, if he had leaped out to stand together with Mizutani and Uragawa in front of Kitami. *Now! Go now!* How many times had he said it to himself? And in spite of all that, he had missed his chance and hadn't gone at all.

I . . . Copper said to himself. *It wasn't that I was scared to jump out. I didn't even think about running away. I just stood there.*

But then, when Kurokawa had said, "Kitami's friends, come forward!"—who was that who had quietly dropped his snowballs?

Copper thought back to that moment. Perhaps nobody else had noticed, but he himself knew what he had done.

The feeling he'd had then! It was like all the blood had drained from his face. Looking around so carefully out of the corner of his eye, just to make sure that nobody had seen!

Copper yearned to banish this memory from his heart. He had betrayed his friends. And no matter what he did, there was no way to undo his cowardly deed.

Oh, he had done a terrible thing! A terrible thing!

Copper hadn't shown much sympathy for his friends or even shed a tear. And now the three boys laughing and chasing him through the snow already somehow seemed a thing of far away and long ago. For some long minutes Copper stood like that, and then he sensed signs of movement from Kitami and the other two boys. Mizutani was saying something, Kitami was nodding, and it seemed they were getting ready to return to the school building.

Yes, the three of them were already going. If he was going to apologize, now was the moment. If he missed this chance . . .

So Copper thought. But still he found himself unable to run over to his friend Kitami. The embarrassment! The shame! His body seemed nailed to the spot. All he could do was tremble and turn his eyes weakly in the direction of the three boys.

"If Kitami would only look this way and smile, even a little bit . . . Or if Mizutani would just say something . . ."

Over and over, Copper prayed for it to happen.

That's right—if Kitami or Mizutani would just do something like that, then he would run to the three of them without another thought. And then he might cry out an apology for what he had done.

However, Kitami and the others just kept walking back to the school building, as if Copper were invisible.

Only Uragawa stopped for a moment and looked back at Copper. When their eyes met, Uragawa made a sympathetic face and seemed like he was going to say something, but that was just for a few seconds, and then in a moment, Uragawa, too, had turned his back to Copper and walked off.

Copper was left all alone.

He had let another chance to apologize get away! He was sorry about that, but more than anything, Copper couldn't stand watching the three of them depart together—such good friends, so close!—while he was left alone, friendless.

Kitami had his arm on Mizutani's shoulder. Mizutani was holding Kitami up, supporting him. And then wasn't Uragawa, too, walking right there next to Kitami?

The three of them had faced the same dangers, suffered and wept together. At that moment, they had truly acted as one. They probably still felt bad about what had happened, but along with those bad feelings, they had the happiness of having friends whom they knew they could believe in.

Copper could imagine how that felt. But all he could do was imagine it, and he must have been miserable that he was not qualified to join this group.

His best friend since elementary school, Mizutani, was leaving with his arm around Kitami, without even looking back at Copper.

Hadn't even Uragawa, who so respected and trusted Copper, now only cast him a mere pitying glance and walked away without a word?

Standing dejectedly in the snow, Copper watched his three friends from behind as they got farther and farther away. As he did, there was a salty taste in his mouth. Hot tears of misery had begun to flow, and finally they blurred the three departing figures beyond recognition.

All strength gone, Copper let his head hang down.

✳

Copper had nearly no memory of how he got home that day.

As he walked through the streets full of melted snow, dragging his umbrella behind him, and sat in a seat on the train, all the day's events floated before his eyes. And whenever he got to the final scene, where his three friends left the schoolyard, fresh tears would well up in Copper's eyes.

Even after he got home, although his mother went to the trouble of making his favorite pancakes, he left them half uneaten. At dinner, too, the food seemed to stick in his throat. His mother was worried.

"Does your stomach hurt?" she asked, but Copper said nothing.

"Are you feeling okay, or are you sick?"

Again, he made no reply.

"What is going on with you? That face!"

Copper's mother put her hand to his forehead. It was as hot as a fire. When she got out the thermometer, he had a real fever. Standing in the snow for such a long time, covered in sweat, Copper must have caught a cold and become truly sick.

His mother sent him straight to bed. She brought him an ice pack for his forehead and had him take aspirin for the fever.

While she was caring for him, Copper hardly opened his mouth. He was feeling pretty bad, it's true, and didn't want to talk. But it wasn't just that. If he had tried to say a friendly word, the dam might have broken and let loose a flood of tears. The kinder his mother was to him, the more he felt that way.

But his mother must have thought that Copper's silence was due to his illness, because after shaking out the night-clothes that she had wrapped him in to soak up his sweat, she turned out the lights, said, "Good night, dear, try to get some rest tonight," and quietly left the room.

Alone in the room, Copper closed his eyes tight.

But when he did, he kept seeing what had happened in the schoolyard. Kurokawa's terrifying face, the look in the eyes of the boy with the shaved head, Kitami collapsed in the snow, and then—and then those three figures, backs turned as they walked away from him.

Copper buried his mouth in the neck of his heavy nightclothes and cried. The teardrops on his pillow would be his own secret.

I've been abandoned by the three of them, he thought. *Now they won't be friends with me. No matter how miserable I am . . .*

Copper couldn't stand it any longer and tossed off his bedclothes. The cold air passed through his pajamas and flowed over him. Although his head was burning hot, his back was shivering from the cold. Each time the chill hit him, he would shake violently, but he didn't cover himself up again.

Let the sickness get worse and worse! Worse and worse, until finally I die . . .

Ah, if only Copper's friends could know how he felt then.

Chapter Seven

Stone-Step Memories

Copper's cold worsened, until eventually he had been sick in bed for two weeks. For a while, his mother started to worry that his illness was developing into pneumonia.

For the first three days, Copper was lost in a painful delirium from dawn to dusk, with a fever of around 40 degrees Celsius. But thanks to his mother's tireless care through the day and night, his fever started to break around the fourth day, and his aches and pains began to recede as well.

A week later, he was well enough to sit up and read, but because of a lingering fever and a cough that he couldn't seem to shake, Copper remained confined to his bed.

Usually when Copper had a little cold such as this had now become, he was all too eager to get back to school. If you tried to keep him in bed, he'd say, "I'm hardly sick at all!" But this time, he obediently followed the doctor's orders, staying meekly in bed. In fact, he was a little too meek, which worried his mother.

What could be wrong? I wonder if anything's happened to him? his mother would sometimes ask herself, with a tilt of her head.

Copper, stuck in bed, thought back to the events of that snowy day. The more he thought about it, the harder it seemed to go back to school and face Kitami and the other boys. Fortunately, he had been sick since then and had to stay home, so until now he had been able to get by without doing so.

But he couldn't go on like this indefinitely. At some point he would have to go back, and he would have to face the three of them. When he thought about what lay ahead, he was understandably uneasy.

Still, he couldn't stand the possibility of never again seeing the three boys. Mizutani, with whom he had been so close; Uragawa, who had trusted him so deeply; and Kitami, who had become such a great friend—it was overwhelming just to think of being turned away by them, those bonds broken forever.

What should I do?

Copper buried his chin in his bedclothes and spent hours staring blankly at the ceiling, plunged deep in thought.

To be honest, facing the three boys would be really hard. But to be friends with them again, the way it was before, was what he wanted most. No, it was what he needed. So there was nothing to do but apologize so that everyone would feel better—this, even Copper could see. But what should he say in his apology?

A number of excuses occurred to Copper, one by one. First, Kitami and Mizutani surely didn't know that when Kitami and his friends had been caught and beaten by the older students, Copper had been watching from the very beginning.

So Copper could say that he had thought something was strange and had come back to see what had happened, but it was only after Kitami and the others had already been beaten. They might believe that.

That's right. If I say that, Kitami probably won't take it badly that I didn't rush to their defense. Because that way, it isn't a question of why I didn't do it. It's that there wasn't even time to jump in if I had wanted . . .

That was his first thought.

But when he considered Uragawa, suddenly Copper was stuck. Uragawa had been among the onlookers. He might know that Copper had been watching from the first. If that was the case, the lie would soon be revealed.

Then what about using his illness as the reason?

At the time of the commotion, I was overcome with chills. I was definitely already getting sick by then, I think. I was feeling bad. I was feeling bad, and I could barely stand up. It was really awful that I couldn't run over there, but it was because I was sick, so please, can you forgive me?

If he said that and apologized, they might gladly forgive him.

But to feel sick so suddenly, right after he had been laughing and carrying on and jumping about like that, well, hardly anyone would believe that. When he thought it over, this excuse, too, was no good.

Well, what about if he said this:

I was about to jump in and join you in front of Kurokawa as we all promised, but then suddenly I had an idea. What if I stayed where I was instead and watched everything really carefully so that afterward I could be a witness? If I did that, the teacher would believe what I said, and Kurokawa and his friends would get punished for sure. So I thought that to avenge Kitami and all of you, it would be better if I waited patiently—even though I wanted to join you—so I could carefully observe the facts. Actually, that's what I was thinking, so I stayed where I was.

Of course! If he said this, he'd appear to be a considerate person, and what's more, he'd have at least a basic explanation for his broken promise.

But would they believe him? It seemed highly unlikely. And what if they did? Copper imagined Kitami apologizing right back at him, saying, *Is that how it happened? We didn't know any of that, so it was wrong of us to think badly of you. Now we're the ones who are sorry.* If that happened, would Copper be able to keep his calm?

No, if that happened, there was no way Copper would be able to take it. Because to do that would really be to deceive his friends.

Even if no one else in the world knew, the memory of that would leave an ugly mark on his heart forever. After all, he himself had listened to Kurokawa shout "Kitami's people, come out now!" and instead he had hidden his snowballs behind his back!

And then he had secretly dropped the snowballs so nobody around would know!

Oh, how could he pretend to be a deep thinker, a great person, with this memory clinging to him? How could he deceive himself?

Copper really began to dislike that person who'd stood there in the snow and abandoned his friends, even though it was Copper himself. He'd never dreamed that he could be so cowardly, so weak when it really counted.

At the same time, he had become keenly aware that a person's conduct was made up of actions that, once done, could not be undone, and that was a truly scary thing. Even if nobody else knew what you'd done, you yourself knew, and what's more, even if you could somehow forget completely, once you'd done a thing, there was no changing that fact. There was absolutely no way afterward to deny to yourself that you were that sort of person.

What should I do? What should I do?

Staring at the ceiling, Copper chewed on his lip. Thinking like this in the darkening room at sundown, with the lights not yet on, he felt an unspeakable loneliness.

Copper had become silent and withdrawn. There had been so many times recently when he was lost in thought.

Usually when Copper was sick, he found ways to enjoy himself as soon as he felt the slightest bit better. When he was sick, his mother would generally do whatever he asked, to whatever extent his illness permitted. It was customary for Copper to make a great show of these sickbed privileges, ordering various things from her.

But this time, on the contrary, whether his mother asked if he wanted an omelet for lunch or some Russian tea cakes for a snack, or if there wasn't some book he'd like to read, all Copper would do was just reply in the most listless way. His mother would try to lift his spirits, talking to him, but before she had said much at all, Copper would end the conversation, saying, "Let's just be quiet for a little while . . ."

And with a gloomy look on his face, he'd roll over, and his mother would be left facing his back. Brows knit with worry, his mother wanted to ask him why, but instead, after a moment, she would quietly stand up and leave. At those times Copper could hear her sigh gently, and with his back still to her, he would weep quietly into his pillow.

This was a real crisis for Copper. He had never before been shaken like this.

When his father had passed away, Copper had been lonely and sad, and often he'd cried. But even then, he hadn't tortured himself with remorse. When he'd given in to the sadness, he'd soon felt better.

But this time, the thought that he had done something that he couldn't undo, no matter how much he regretted it, was hurting him over and over again. Often he would wake suddenly in the middle of the night and lie there, eyes wide open, unable to sleep.

For the first time, Copper knew what it was like to examine his own thoughts and actions, carefully and closely.

How many days passed like this one!

Before he knew it, Copper's mood had become somber.

No matter how he tried to cover up what he had done, there was no changing the fact that he had betrayed his own friends. That would follow Copper everywhere and be fixed forever in his conscience.

Copper had stopped trying to think up excuses. He was just deeply saddened by what he had done to Kitami and Mizutani and Uragawa, and felt that it was truly unforgivable. And at that point his mood began to shift. He wanted to apologize honestly to the three of them, to tell them that he had been wrong.

But would they forgive him just because he apologized? If Copper owned up to his own cowardice, wouldn't that make the three of them all the more disgusted with him?

When he thought that, of course, he couldn't help but be torn.

It was Sunday afternoon.

The sun was shining brightly through the paper panels of the sliding shoji doors, and the hiss of boiling water rose repeatedly from the iron kettle on the hibachi. Next to Copper, his uncle was lounging, silently reading the newspaper.

Copper was lying on his back. The lukewarm ice pack that he no longer needed hung limp and mushy from its hook on the stand near his bed. He poked at it, rocking it gently like a swing at a playground. It moved like a piston, first one way and back, then the other way and back, but all the while Copper was thinking of something else altogether.

Should I say something? Or shouldn't I . . . ?

If he was going to say anything, now was the right time, when it was just the two of them alone. For a long time he wavered, but finally, Copper opened his mouth.

"Say, Uncle."

"Yes, what is it?"

His uncle didn't lift his eyes from the newspaper.

"I, well . . ."

"Yes?"

"I . . ."

Having started, Copper was unable to continue. Although he had finally made up his mind to speak to his uncle, once the moment came, it was hard to get the words out. But he pressed on and spoke.

"I don't want to go back to school."

His uncle was surprised by Copper's tormented tone and looked up from the newspaper.

"Why not?

"I . . . Because I don't want to go back." Copper repeated himself, sounding almost angry.

"So you said, but you're almost fully recovered, and isn't it time for exams?"

"Even so. I don't want to go anyway."

"Why?"

"Because I . . ." Again, Copper choked on his words.

"That's strange, isn't it? Usually, you—"

"No—!"

Copper interrupted, shaking his head violently.

"Uncle, I, well . . ."

When he started again, suddenly his eyes became hot, and then the tears started to flow. He felt like he was choking, but again Copper spoke.

"I . . . I did a really unforgivable thing."

His uncle sat up and gave Copper a long look. Copper was still lying down, and tears ran from the corner of his eye, painting a line down toward his ear.

"What in the world was it?" His uncle spoke quietly. "Can't you tell your uncle?"

Looking at Copper, who was staring at the ceiling through his tears and unable to reply, his uncle spoke again.

"Well, you know it's okay to tell it all to me, whatever it is."

Haltingly, Copper told his uncle of the promise they had all made at Mizutani's house during the New Year's holiday, of the events of the snowy day, and how his three friends had all turned their backs on him. While he was speaking, he felt all the things that had been bottled up so tightly inside him finally flowing out. By the end of the story, he was able to speak relatively smoothly again.

"Uncle, I think I did something really bad. I think Kitami and all of them must be really mad at me, and I don't think there's anything I can do about it. I acted like a coward. A coward."

When he had finished, Copper felt like a great burden had been lifted from his shoulders.

"Is that right? That's all that happened?" His uncle, too, sounded somewhat relieved. "Then, Copper, what do you think you should do?"

"I don't know what to do. I just want Kitami and all of them to understand."

"Understand what?"

"To understand . . . what I did, it was wrong. But I think that it's really unforgivable. Right now, right now when I think of it, I can't stand it!"

"Go on."

"And on top of that, Uncle, this is not an excuse, but over and over I was thinking that I would run out in front of Kurokawa!"

His uncle didn't respond.

"It's true, Uncle! I was really thinking I should go join them. I thought and thought, but I didn't make up my mind, and while I was hesitating, Kitami got beaten up. I was afraid and didn't help them, but I was really worried about them. I wasn't just watching them calmly! I just want them to know that."

"Yes, that's understandable." His uncle sympathized.

"What should I do?"

His uncle replied briskly, in an attempt to encourage Copper.

"That? You hardly need to think about that at all, do you? You should write a letter immediately. Write a letter, and apologize to Kitami. This is not something to carry around with you in your heart forever!"

Copper hesitated.

"But, Uncle, if I do that, will Kitami and the rest of them feel better about me?"

"That, I don't know."

"Then I don't want to."

At that, his uncle suddenly gave him a sharp look.

"Jun'ichi!"

Copper's uncle dropped his affectionate nickname and spoke sternly.

"It's a mistake to think that way! You broke a solemn promise to your close friends, didn't you? Weren't you unable to stand by Kitami and the others because you were afraid of Kurokawa's fists? You said yourself that you think you were in the wrong, and that it couldn't be helped if they were angry with you. Why in the world would you say such a thing? Why don't you be brave and take responsibility for what you did, as far as you are able?"

Copper felt as if he had been lashed with a whip. Regardless, his uncle continued in a severe tone.

"You can't complain that you were abandoned by Kitami and Mizutani. You should have nothing to say about that whatsoever!"

Copper shut his eyes tight, his face mournful beyond words.

"Well. To part with such good friends over something like this is a painful state of affairs," his uncle said, returning to a quieter tone of voice.

"I understand the feeling you expressed, that you want to mend your relationship with Kitami and the others. But you must understand, Copper, that you can't think of that right now. What you must do now, before anything else, is first to apologize to Kitami like a man. To convey to your friends how deeply sorry you are feeling and to do it honestly, without excuses. What happens after that is not for you to think about now.

"If you humbly admit your mistake, that may help you make amends with Kitami and the others, and perhaps you can all be friends as before. Or else they may remain resentful and continue to turn their backs on you. That is something you can't know here and now, no matter how much you try to think it through. However, even if they do reject your friendship, you can't complain.

"That's why—you see, Copper—that's why now is the moment to show courage! You must resolve to face the consequences of your actions with bravery, whatever they may be, no matter how hard!

"When you think about it, your failure before was due to your inability to show such resolve, wasn't it? Didn't you lack the courage to keep the solemn promise you made?"

Eyes still tightly shut, Copper nodded silently.

"You must not repeat this mistake again. Gather your courage, Copper, and do what you must do. No matter what you do, you can't change the past. Think of the present instead. Go and do what you have to do now, and be brave. When it comes to this sort of thing—Copper, when it comes to this sort of thing, you simply must not give in.

"So pull yourself together, and write the letter to Kitami. Write your feelings honestly, and beg forgiveness from Kitami and the others. If you do that, you may come to feel some sense of relief."

Copper listened to his uncle's words without speaking but this time opened his eyes, wet with tears, gazed off into space without looking his uncle in the face, and spoke earnestly.

"Uncle! I'll write the letter."

And then, almost as if to himself, he added, "If Kitami and the others don't forgive me, I'll . . . I'll wait until they do."

That afternoon, it took Copper a good long while, but he wrote a letter to Kitami.

To: Kitami Kouta
March XX

Dear Kitami,
When you were caught by Kurokawa's friends, having such a hard time, I was there. I was watching silently the whole time. Mizutani and Uragawa didn't run or hide, and I watched them go through the same hard time together with you. But I didn't come forward.

I didn't forget that I swore to stand with you if you were attacked.

I remembered that perfectly. But still, I didn't keep my promise. I think what I did was really, really cowardly.

I don't know what to say to apologize to you. You can't know how ashamed I am that I behaved in such an unforgivable way to you, to Mizutani, and to Uragawa. When I think of it, I am so full of feelings that I don't know what to do.

I feel like a coward, or spineless, or whatever kind of hopeless person you want to call it.

If you hate me or don't want to talk to me anymore, I have no right to say a word.

Only, I believe what I did was wrong, and feel so, so sorry that I can't stand it. I think I would rather be dead. I just want you, please, to understand somehow that I know how bad I was.

I wasn't brave, and I didn't come out to support you. But I never felt for a second that I didn't care about you.

I feel the same now. I want you to understand my feelings someday. At the least, I definitely want that. This time, I promise I will try to be brave.

If you can, please try to believe that.

If you believe that, I will be happy beyond words.

Your friend,
Honda Jun'ichi

P.S. Please show this letter to Mizutani and Uragawa.

When he finished the letter, Copper called the maid and gave it to her to mail as soon as possible. Then he gathered up all the pages covered with his earlier mistakes, tore these into small pieces, stuffed them in the wastepaper basket, and after straightening up the bedside, lay down in bed. When he had done that, a feeling that was neither exhaustion nor peace of mind became a deep sigh, and he let it out. Copper felt that for the moment at least, the forces that had been straining him to the breaking point had relaxed their hold, and limply, he closed his eyes.

He had the feeling he could hear a voice coming faintly from somewhere, saying, "It's okay, it's okay."

Copper wasn't thinking anything anymore. Only trying to catch that faint faraway voice, while his whole body drifted closer and closer to a deep, deep sleep . . .

The following day the weather was fine once again.

The south-facing shoji door was full of sunlight, brightening the inside of the room, and the iron kettle continued its quiet nonstop monologue.

Copper was in bed reading a school textbook. His plan was to catch up little by little on the parts he had missed while he was away. However, before he'd finish even a page, his eyes would wander from the book, through the glass of the sliding door, and soar off into the splendid clear sky outside.

I wonder if that letter reached Kitami's place yesterday evening. If it did, Kitami will surely be taking it to school today to show to Mizutani and Uragawa. But then again, maybe it didn't arrive yesterday. If not, then Kitami probably hasn't read it yet, but . . .

Over and over, these thoughts rolled around in Copper's head. But every time he realized he was daydreaming, Copper would shut down his imagination, return to his textbook, and try not to be distracted by anything else.

Whenever he drifted back to these thoughts—imagining what Kitami would think of the letter once he had read it, what Mizutani and Uragawa would say, and whether they would all feel better about things—Copper was drawn back to the suffocating feelings he'd had before he wrote the letter. *No good, no good! It's no good to think of that now,* Copper told himself and tried not to think any further ahead.

Yes, that's right. Regarding the mistakes he had made, Copper had already thought everything he could think, regretted as much as he could regret, suffered all there was to suffer. Now he needed to face straight forward and think about how to live his life properly from now on.

"You're studying today?"

Hearing his mother's voice, he looked over and saw her standing, holding a vase in which she had arranged some peach blossoms.

"Pretty, aren't they?"

Copper smiled warmly and nodded. From the vase that she held to her chest, peach branches spread freely in all directions, half-hiding her face, some flowers just opening and others still in bud, and blossoms scattering everywhere in a deep, dewy crimson. To Copper, the swelling blossoms seemed much more than pretty.

Copper's mother placed the vase in an alcove, sat herself down next to Copper, and started her knitting. Copper started reading his textbook again. The two of them continued like that in the quiet room for some time, hardly saying a word while the iron kettle bubbled gently.

During that time, when Copper again started to stare off into the sky, his mother began to speak: "Jun'ichi, when your mother knits, there is something I often think of."

She spoke slowly, in a gentle voice.

"Well, I'll tell you. It's a story from when I was in high school. Often I would make a side trip on the way home from school, going down by the old Tenjin shrine in Yushima and then passing through its grounds on the way back to our house in Hongo. At those times, I used to make a habit of walking up the stone staircase behind the shrine and coming out through the precinct garden.

"You know, Jun'ichi, I think that old stone staircase might be standing there even now, right there behind the shrine. They were the sort of lonely stone steps that would make you shiver if you walked there, even at midday. I wonder what it's like there now . . .

"One day when your mother was climbing those stone steps, it so happened that there was an old woman climbing the staircase, just five or six steps ahead of me, a bundle wrapped in a cotton cloth hanging from one hand.

"That's right, she must have been more than seventy years old, I think. I remember her even now. She was a little old granny, her gray hair cut short and loose, wearing a narrow satin belt tied flat around her kimono. She had the hem of the kimono tucked up, her skinny legs with white *tabi* socks stuck out from underneath her white waistcoat, and she was using an umbrella as a cane to help heave herself up the steep stone staircase.

"I couldn't tell what was in her bundle, but it seemed really heavy for something so small. She was wearing *geta* sandals, and as she worked her way carefully up each stone step, the tall wooden teeth of the sandals clattered against the stone, and even though she was watching her footing, her every step was unsteady. She would climb two or three steps, then rest, climb again, then rest, and with each rest she would stretch her legs and then, again, heaving and straining, continue to climb. I could hardly bring myself to watch it.

"Well, I thought, I have to carry that bag for her. It would be easy enough to dash up the stairs and catch the old woman, and no great effort to carry her bag and even to take the woman's arm and help her climb.

"So when the woman stopped, about halfway up, to catch her breath and stretch, I thought I'd run up to her side. But just at that moment, she set out walking again. Once she started moving, her back hunched over, as if the climb demanded every ounce of her attention, I felt it wasn't a good time to call out to her, and somehow I couldn't just run up to her like that, so instead I just continued to climb silently behind her.

"As I followed in her footsteps, I told myself that the next time the woman took a break, I'd run to her and speak up, saying, *Granny, please let me carry that for you!*

"But the next time she stopped, I felt awkward for some reason and didn't move right away. While I was wondering what to do, the grandmother finally started to climb the stone steps again, without so much as a look back.

"*The next time she stops—* So I thought and again went climbing a few steps behind the old woman. But the next time, too, I hesitated a little and missed my chance, and again it was too late.

"This happened two or perhaps three more times. Anyway, there weren't that many more steps, and the woman eventually reached the top of the stairs. At that time, I followed right behind, hesitating and hesitating again, until the two of us took our last steps and stood there together in the Tenjin-sama precincts.

"The old woman reached the top of the stairs, never dreaming I was right behind her, worrying myself with these thoughts. She lowered her heavy bundle onto a nearby stone bench, and for a while, as if she had completely forgotten to sit down herself, looked down over the town below, leaning on her umbrella and breathing deeply, shoulders heaving.

"And when I walked by, she glanced in my direction briefly but then quickly turned away again, looking not particularly interested. And in spite of that, it's strange, you know, but for my part, I remember her face perfectly even now!

"Jun'ichi, dear. That's all there is to the story. But even all these years later, I still sometimes remember what happened then. Yes, I remember all sorts of feelings, at all sorts of times."

Copper's mother became quiet for a while. And then, while her hands busied themselves with her knitting needles, she seemed to be remembering some far-off thing, but presently, quietly, she began to speak again.

"I couldn't help but notice the old woman's weary state, and while I thought that I should carry her heavy bag for her, I only thought so deep inside and in the end was unable to do it—well, the story is just that, but it made a strangely deep impression on my heart.

"Even then, when I left the woman, I was thinking all sorts of things on my way home. Why didn't I run to her side when we stopped? Why didn't I do what I had been thinking inside? I began to feel like I had done a very bad thing.

"Besides, once we had gotten to the top of the stairs, my good intentions didn't matter at all. The chance to do what I had felt in my heart probably wasn't going to come a second time. That chance—well, dear, that opportunity was gone forever the moment that woman reached the top step, wasn't it? It was really a small thing, but still, I regretted it all the same. Later, no matter how often I thought about it, it was too late to go back and fix it. If you can't go back, a small thing like this is not different in the least from a big irreversible event.

"Isn't that right, dear? It's already been so many years since then. I must have been a fourth-year student at the girls' school then, so it's already been more than twenty years, hasn't it? And then I grew up and married your father, and we were together until you were born, Jun'ichi, and much longer, until the year before last, when he passed away. During those twenty years, a lot has happened.

"And still, when it comes to this memory of the stone staircase, I remember it clearly, as if it were yesterday. If you ask me why, I think it's because I thought about that time so often, while going through so many things.

"Jun'ichi, dear. Even when we become adults, it often happens that we think back on things with regret. We wonder, *Why didn't I do what was in my heart that one time?* When just about anyone takes a serious look back at their lives, we all may have one or two things like this.

"The older we get, the bigger the things are, the harder they are to take back, and the more we feel this way, compared to when we were children.

"Since your father passed away, I always find myself thinking *Oh, if only I had done this* or *If only I had done that.*"

Copper's mother set down her knitting and stilled her hands, and together with Copper she looked for a while at the clear aqua sky through the window, but then putting on a bright face, as if pulling herself together, she smiled and continued.

"But, Jun'ichi, the memory of the stone staircase is not a bad memory for me.

"What I mean is, there have often been times since then when I felt sorry for something I did, and wished that I had behaved differently, but it's not as if I never felt truly glad I did something either. These aren't the sorts of things where we stop to think how it will work out for us personally. We act to show the warm and beautiful things we feel in our hearts, just as they are, and after that, we might have a brief moment now and then when we think, *Oh, I'm glad I did that.*

"And when I think about those moments now, they all seem to be thanks to the memories of those stone steps.

"It's really true, you know. Without the memory of those stone steps, I wouldn't have been able to encourage the good and beautiful things in my own heart to grow to become what they are now. If I didn't have that memory, I might not have realized for a long time after how each and every event in our lives happens once only and will never be repeated. How we have to work to nurture that which is good and beautiful in our own hearts.

"So I think that what happened on those stone steps was not a loss. I was sorry, but I also learned something essential about how to live. And also, I learned to deeply appreciate the kindness of others."

Copper's mother's words connected strongly with the sharp pangs of regret he had been feeling recently, and slowly he came to understand very well what she was saying.

"So then, Jun'ichi—" his mother said, taking up her knitting again and looking him in the face.

"Jun'ichi, dear, it's possible that sometime you, too, may experience something like what happened to your mother. If it comes to that, it may even be something much, much harder than what I experienced, and you will know what it feels like to regret something.

"But, Jun'ichi, if that should happen, it will never be to your loss! If you think only of that one thing, you'll never be able to change it, but if your regrets help you to really learn an essential thing about being human, that experience won't have been wasted on you. Your life afterward, thanks to that, will be better and stronger than it was before. Jun'ichi, that's the only way for a person to become great.

"So please never give up hope in yourself! Then, when that future Jun'ichi gets back on his feet, the great things about him—well, someone will surely notice them.

"Even when people don't notice, the gods are certainly watching and will know."

As Copper listened to his mother's words, his eyes became a little misty. He wondered if possibly his mother had heard about his recent trouble from his uncle.

His mother who, even though she knew all about it, told her story without mentioning his struggle! His mother who so casually and carefully worked to cheer him up!

Copper tried hard to hold back his tears, but they welled up and spilled out. These were completely different tears from the ones that Copper had cried and cried recently.

The warm sky on the other side of the window was calm and clear and already seemed like spring.

On Human Troubles, Mistakes, and Greatness

Human beings are so great that they demonstrate their greatness by recognizing their own misery. A tree does not recognize that it is miserable.

Of course, it is true that "it is miserable to recognize oneself as miserable," but then again it is also similarly true that it is greatness itself to recognize oneself as miserable.

Thus human misery proves the greatness of all human beings.

It is the misery of a king who has lost his throne.

... Other than a dethroned king, who among
us would feel sadness in not being a king? ...
Who would feel unlucky to have only one mouth?
Moreover, who would not feel unlucky to have
only one eye? No one who lived would ever think
it sad that they had not three eyes, but if they had
but one, they would be beyond consolation.

—Blaise Pascal

If a rightful ruler loses his throne, he will think himself unfortunate and be sad that he has no throne. He will be sad for his present self, because he who should have a throne now has none.

Similarly, a one-eyed man also feels unfortunate, because although we expect human beings to be born with two eyes, he lacks that. If people naturally had only one eye, you can be sure that nobody would be crying over being one-eyed. No, on the contrary, people who had been born with two eyes would be crying at the thought of being deformed.

Copper, we must try to think deeply about this. There are important truths to be found here. They can teach us much about the meaning of human sadness and suffering.

As we move through our lives as human beings, all of us, young and old, encounter sadness, hardship, and pain, each in our own way.

Of course, those are not things anyone ever wishes for. But

it is thanks to sadness, hardship, and pain that we come to know what a true human being is.

This is not limited to the pain and suffering that one feels in one's heart. Likewise, the pain and suffering that we feel right in our bodies hold the same sort of meaning.

In good health, when nothing is wrong in our bodies, we live our lives almost forgetting that a heart, a stomach, intestines, and all the many other organs are inside us, playing an important role in our everyday lives. However, when something goes wrong and our heart skips or our stomach hurts, then for the first time we think about our own organs and become aware of the problem. When we feel physical pain or suffering, it's because something has gone wrong, and it's thanks to that pain and suffering that we realize that.

You could say that when we feel pain, the pain is telling us that conditions are not normal in our bodies. If we didn't feel any pain at all, even when something went wrong, we might not realize it, and depending on the circumstances, that might cost us our lives.

In fact, even in the case of a bad tooth, if there's no pain, the treatment is much more likely to be delayed, while the cavity quickly grows, than if it hurts.

So although there's no doubt that everyone wants to avoid physical pain, in this sense, it's something that we should be grateful for, something we need. Because of it, we know that a failure has occurred inside us, and at the same time, we also come to know exactly what the natural state of the human body should be.

In the same way, when a person is living in a way that's not normal for a human being, suffering and hardships of the heart let us know that. So then, thanks to that pain and suffering, we can clearly grasp what a human being should naturally be.

If it weren't natural for people to live together in harmony, then why would we suffer when we felt a lack of harmony? If we should try to live a life of love and goodwill toward others but instead find ourselves driven by hatred and hostility, we feel unfortunate because of that, and for that reason, we suffer.

Furthermore, anyone should be able to cultivate their own talents and to work according to those talents, so people suffer when they can't do that, and feel they can hardly endure it.

People feel sad and suffer like this because it's not natural to have such hatred and hostility toward each other. Also, because it's wrong that they cannot freely cultivate the talents with which they were born.

Generally, when people feel they are miserable, when people suffer, it's because that kind of misery isn't natural.

Copper, we must find a way to draw knowledge from all our suffering and sadness!

Of course, there are also people who *believe* that they are unfortunate, because their own selfish desires haven't been gratified. Others go through various hardships for the sake of the most superficial vanities.

However, the suffering and unhappiness of these sorts of people actually happens because they can't let go of their selfish desires, their trivial vanities. If they do find a way to let such things go, they find that the pain vanishes at the same time.

Again, a truth lies concealed under this unhappiness and pain—that people need not hold on to such desires or vanities.

Naturally, pain is not unique to human beings. Even dogs and cats may shed tears if wounded, and when they are lonely, they howl piteously. When it comes to physical pain or hunger or thirst, humans are surely the same as other animals. That's why we experience a keen sense of empathy and feel great affection for other living creatures on the planet, be they dogs, cats, horses, or cows. But that also means that pain alone tells us little about what it means to be truly human.

We learn true humanity from a pain that only humans feel, even in the midst of experiencing all the same pain as other living things.

So then, what sort of thing is this unique pain so special to humanity?

Even if our bodies have not been injured or starved, people can feel wounded, starving, and thirsty.

If our dreams are cruelly dashed, then our hearts are wounded and invisible blood flows. If we must live without kindness and affection, our hearts develop an unquenchable thirst.

But among all those miseries, there's one that pierces our hearts most deeply, that wrings the bitterest tears from our eyes. It's the awareness that we have committed a mistake that we can't go back and fix. When we look back on our actions—not in terms of personal benefit but in a moral frame of mind—I'm afraid there's nothing quite so painful as thinking, *What have I done?*

That's it. It's truly painful to admit one's own mistakes. Most people think up any excuse they can to avoid it.

However, Copper, when you have made a mistake, to recognize it bravely and to suffer for it is something that in all of heaven and earth, only humans can do.

If people didn't naturally know the right thing to do, and hold the power to determine their own conduct with that as a foundation, then wouldn't it be nearly meaningless to reflect on what one has done and regret one's mistakes?

It's because we think *I didn't have to do that* or *It was within my power to do this* that we are battered by feelings of regret. If we didn't have the power to follow the voice of reason, why would we taste the pain of remorse?

It's hard to admit our mistakes. But in the pain of our mistakes there is also human greatness.

"Other than a dethroned king, who would sorrow over not having a throne?"

If we were not born with the ability to conduct ourselves with morality, there would be no reason for bitter tears.

As long as we are human, we all make mistakes. And then, as long as our conscience doesn't go numb, the knowledge of the mistakes we have made can't help but cause painful thoughts for all of us.

However, Copper, can't we always draw fresh confidence from these painful thoughts in return? After all, it's because we have the power to walk the path of justice that we also experience this pain.

"Error has the same relationship to truth as sleeping does to waking. I have seen that when one wakes from error, one turns to truth again as if revived."

These are the words of Goethe.

We have the power to decide on our own who we will be.

Therefore, we will make mistakes.

However—

We have the power to decide on our own who we will be.

Therefore, we can also recover from mistakes.

And finally, Copper, if you want to know where the motion of your "human particles" differs from the motion of other particles, this is it!

~~~~~~

Chapter Eight

A Triumphant Return

The day after listening to his mother's story, Copper got up from bed. He was well again. The doctor said that he could return to school in two or three days. Free from confinement for the first time in two long weeks, Copper roamed restlessly around inside the house, until the third day after sending the letter to Kitami arrived.

What would Kitami's answer be? Copper had already made up his mind not to worry about it, but he was looking forward to a response. When the time for postal delivery drew near, he developed a sudden interest in the mailbox on the front gate, now and then going to take a casual peek.

But even after three days, there was no reply from Kitami.

It was the afternoon of the fourth day.

Copper was trimming his toenails in the warm and sunny second-floor hallway when his mother came pattering up the steep staircase on unusually hurried legs.

"Jun'ichi, dear, you have a visitor!"

His mother called out to Copper before she had reached the top of the stairs. Then, with a joyful look, she bounded across the room to Copper and said, a little breathlessly, "It's Kitami! Kitami came! Mizutani and Uragawa, too—"

"Huh?" Copper's eyes widened. "Mother, really?"

"It's true! Really, they came. Quick, come down to the front hall."

Copper jumped up, forgetting everything else. Without even a glance at his mother, he leaped across the hallway in a single bound and flew down the staircase. He didn't even realize he was still holding the nail clipper in his hand.

He ran to the front hall, and there were his three friends, standing in a row on the concrete floor. There were their three faces, all jumbled together in front of him, one after another. Kitami was smiling. Mizutani was smiling. Uragawa was smiling. The three looked at Copper, fond grins on their faces.

"Hi!" Kitami called out in a cheerful voice, catching sight of Copper coming toward them. It was a voice bright enough to drive away Copper's two weeks of gloomy feelings in a single stroke. Together with that voice, Copper felt the noisy playground air of the schoolyard rush all at once into the narrow hallway, as if it were crowded with hundreds of students milling about in play.

"Are you all better now?" Kitami spoke up, although Copper hadn't yet come to a stop in front of him.

"All better, thanks," Copper happily replied, arriving by his friends.

"When did you get out of bed?" Mizutani asked.

"The day before yesterday."

"Then you can come back to school, right?" This time it was Uragawa.

"Yes, I think I can go the day after tomorrow."

As he answered bit by bit, Copper felt his own face quickly brightening. It was as if with each reply his body became noticeably lighter, until he was almost floating.

For a while the four of them were busy with questions and answers about Copper's illness, and then for some reason, they all lapsed into silence. They didn't know what to talk about next.

No, they knew what was coming. They just didn't know how to begin.

It was the first time that Copper had seen his three friends since the snowy day, so he felt it would be bad not to start with some words of apology. Kitami and the others, too, felt as if they ought to say something special about Copper's letter. But looking at each other face-to-face like this, why bother? One could see from Kitami's first words that he and his friends were no longer concerned about it. And Copper, too, was aware of this—it was written all over his face.

Copper and the three boys stood there for a moment in silence, grinning briefly for no reason every so often when their eyes met.

"But all of you . . . Why today?" Copper began at last, looking for a way to start.

"Why what?"

"I mean, today, isn't it a school day?"

"Oh, that's right. School let out early today. The teachers have some sort of meeting. Teachers were coming from schools all over the place!"

Kitami replied on behalf of everyone. Then he continued, easily.

"About your letter—it came three days ago. Then I showed it to Mizutani and Uragawa the day before yesterday, and we all said we should write a reply. Then yesterday we found out that we were getting out early today, so we decided, well, let's give up on the letter and all go together."

Copper listened, as one might expect, with his eyes downcast. Kitami spoke.

"All that stuff—don't worry about it. It's fine! We're done thinking about it. Right, Mizutani?"

"Yes," Mizutani replied and addressed Copper. "Jun'ichi, it's really okay not to worry about it. It's not good for you to worry as much as all that."

"But I . . ."

When Copper tried to speak, Uragawa interrupted.

"We said it's okay, Copper! We didn't send you a get-well card either. But there was a big fuss after all that!"

"A very big fuss!" Kitami added. And then the three boys, talking in turns, told him what had happened after the incident of the snowy day.

When you hear about it, you will see that it was indeed a great big fuss.

Hearing that Mizutani and Kitami had been treated roughly, Mizutani's sister had flown into a fury. That day, she stayed up until late in the evening and reported on the incident to their father when he arrived home. She asked him if he would please go to the school and negotiate, no matter what happened.

Their father tried to explain that he had company responsibilities for the next two days, so it wouldn't be possible, but Katsuko would hear nothing of it, and eventually Mr. Mizutani agreed to visit the school on the following day to speak on behalf of the boys.

At Kitami's house, his father was furious. Mr. Kitami was a colonel in the army reserves, and when he heard the story, he said he was going to take Kitami out of the school. It was wrong of Kitami, he said, to forget the proper attitude of younger students toward their seniors. However, to punish someone for that was the teacher's job, and students didn't have that authority, even if they were older. Seeing that Kitami had been in the wrong, he said, Kitami would have to live with the beating he received, but still, the school had no right to look the other way and ignore the senior students who broke the rules.

That was Mr. Kitami's opinion. If the school was going to let the senior students off the hook like this, then there was no reason to entrust them with his son's care, so he would pull Kitami out. So he burst into the school, yelling about this.

At Uragawa's house, his mother was angrier than his father. "Even if he is the son of a poor tofu seller," she said, "he's still an important son to me. He may be stupid and incapable and maybe he did something wrong, but he doesn't deserve this! Are the rich kids the only ones who matter in this school? I'm not going to put up with this kind of injustice!"

Uragawa's mother got ahold of his father and, as if it were his fault entirely, let all her fury out on him. Then he, too, headed off to the school the next day, to ask the teacher what all the fuss was about.

The teachers at the school were all quite surprised to get complaints from three families at the same time. Since it concerned the fifth-year students, who were just then in the midst of their graduation preparations, the teachers were inclined to treat them leniently, but a problem like this couldn't be overlooked.

Kurokawa and his group were called before the teachers, and the facts were examined as usual. Then, although they tried to keep it quiet, news traveled quickly among the students, and for the moment, this was all anyone at school talked about when they got together.

It seemed the teachers as well had much to discuss, but after a week had passed, finally a punishment was handed down. Kurokawa and Shavehead received three days' suspension each. Then the gang of Kurokawa's friends who had pelted Copper's friends with snow were all reprimanded.

A reprimand meant they were called before the headmaster and scolded. After announcing the punishment, the headmaster called a special meeting for all the students in the auditorium and carefully admonished them that there should be no misunderstandings about these events.

It was a great fuss, unequaled in recent years.

The most bewildered of all was Kitami. He told his father the story of what had happened, and in return was told, "You were not in the right either. Until this thing is cleared up, you're grounded!" Given that it was Kitami's father, that was perhaps to be expected. He was a strong-willed, obstinate man, and once he had uttered something, he would absolutely never, under any circumstances, take it back.

No matter how Kitami begged to be allowed back to school, his father refused, saying only, "When I say no, I mean no." In the end Kitami was stuck at home for a week, until the incident had blown over.

"Because of that, even though we heard from the teacher you were sick, we couldn't really come to visit you," Kitami explained. "We didn't know what would happen until everything was settled, so somehow we couldn't even write a letter!"

At that point, Copper's mother, who had been standing silently beside the four boys as they spoke together so intently, cut in: "Jun'ichi, why don't you take your guests to your room, instead of making them stand down here for all this talk?"

"Right, right, I wasn't thinking. Do you all want to come up?"

But Kitami and his friends couldn't stay long. When

Copper asked why, the reason was that Mizutani's sister was waiting for them at the train station.

"Katsuko? Why is she at our station?" Copper asked, surprised. Mizutani explained that Katsuko had graduated from high school and was picking up the entrance guidelines for a women's college in Copper's neighborhood. The four of them had all come together, but she had gone around to the college on her own. They had all made a plan to meet back at the station and return together.

After explaining this, Mizutani turned slightly red-faced.

"Right, so, I, um, have a letter from my sister."

At this he fished an aqua-colored envelope out of his pocket. It was a letter from Katsuko to Copper. Copper opened the envelope immediately.

To: Honda Jun'ichi
March XX

Dear Copper,
How are you feeling? I heard that you were very sick at one point, and I was worried about you.

Yesterday, my brother showed me a letter that you sent to Kitami. That was because Kitami gave him permission to take it home.

When I read that letter, I was very moved. I thought that my little brother is lucky to have a person this conscientious as a friend.

To be honest, when I heard that you didn't stand together with everyone that one time, I was pretty mad at first. Because you had promised to do it, I was thinking. But by the time I finished your letter, I had forgotten all those thoughts. I cried while I was reading it.

I ask you, on behalf of my brother, please don't let what happened cause a strain on your friendship, and I hope that from now on, as before, you and he will be friends for a long time.

Please take good care of yourself.
Katsuko

Copper's hands trembled as he read.

"So Katsuko is waiting at the train station?" Copper asked Mizutani, with a small tremor in his voice.

"Yes, she might be there already."

"Do you think it would be okay to ask her to come to our house?"

"Well, it's fine with me, but she's shy!"

Hearing that, Copper looked back at his mother.

"Mother, is it okay to invite Mizutani's sister as well?"

"Yes, yes, that's fine! If it's no trouble to her, of course we'd love to have her."

"Well then, I'm going to go to the station and invite her! That's okay, right, Mom?"

"Yes, well . . ." his mother said, remembering that Copper was still recovering from his illness, and considering for a bit, but presently, she spoke as if she had made up her mind.

"It should be okay. Go ahead. But put on a cloak, and be sure to wear a scarf!"

Before his mother had finished speaking, Copper had run back upstairs. Returning with a scarf, he made a flying leap at his cloak, which was hanging in the front hall.

"Okay, I'll be right back!"

Copper asked Kitami and his other friends to come with him. Copper's mother turned to the three boys and asked if they'd rather wait at the house, but of course they chose to go together with Copper.

"Come home soon, Jun'ichi. On the way home, please take a taxi from the station!" His mother's words echoing behind him, Copper had already slipped into his wooden *geta* sandals and was clattering out the door.

And before too long, the four young men and Katsuko were riding to Copper's house in one of the station taxis. The car slipped merrily onward, past fields and beneath the branches of the enoki trees set in rows along the roadside.

"Say, Copper . . ." Katsuko was seated next to Copper in the car. "Did you show my letter to your mother?"

"Nope, not yet."

"You can't show her! Although I thought you might, so I used my most polite language."

"If you were polite, isn't it okay to show her?" Copper asked.

"It's not! I wrote that letter to you, not to your mother."

"But that's—I mean, didn't you read the letter that I wrote to Kitami?"

"Well . . . !"

Everyone laughed. The car continued to run onward through the bright sunshine, laughing voices floating out of its windows in all directions. Ahead of them, the white road extended off into the distance, and at the end of it, a tiled rooftop shone warmly, bathed in sunlight.

The hedges flowed steadily alongside them on the right and left, and the tiled rooftop drew gradually nearer. Just after the turn by the tile roof was Copper's house.

Somehow, Copper felt like a general making his triumphant return at the end of a war.

Chapter Nine

Daffodils and Buddhas

C opper and his friends were together again.

His letter had certainly helped, but as it turned out, the three boys had, from the start, not taken things as seriously as Copper had thought they would.

But none of that mattered now. Maybe Copper hadn't needed to spend so many lonely days doubting and worrying, but still, as a result, he was learning how to look at his own actions and thoughts—his own way of life—closely and carefully.

If you think about it, there are sayings such as "Know thyself" and "Reflect upon your past" that we have heard over and over, ever since elementary school. They may feel a bit trite or old-fashioned, and when we hear them now, we may just think, *Oh, that old saw again!*

And Copper had long known the exact meaning of the words of those sayings. If he had to explain what they meant on a test, he would probably get a perfect score.

But just knowing the meaning of the words was a very different thing from grasping the truth expressed by those words. Copper had only recently, little by little, begun to know what it meant to reflect on his life.

In the things Copper did and the things he said, strangely adult moments and still-childish ones were all mixed together, one following the other. But that may be only natural. Copper was almost in the spring of his fifteenth year, and he was transforming day by day from a child to an adult.

And Copper realized that. The baseball bats that the adult players used were too heavy for him to take a full swing, but the bat that his father had bought him when he was in elementary school was oddly light and short in his hands, and he often felt silly waving it around.

Anyway, Copper was changing. And it seemed his uncle had noticed as well. Once Copper had finished his final exams and was looking forward to his second year of junior high school, his uncle gave him the famous maroon notebook, along with a request that Copper carefully read the many notes that his uncle had been writing to him for such a long time.

Today was the day of the spring equinox, in the middle of the week of the Buddhist Higan celebration.

At the front of the small Buddhist altar that sits on a shelf in nearly every Japanese home sat a photograph of Copper's deceased father, and in front of that, there was an expansive arrangement of flowers and fruit. The altar, which was usually so inconspicuous, overflowed with brilliant colors.

Copper was lying on his stomach in front of it, deep in thought, a brand-new hand-bound notebook open before him. The notebook was one that his mother had chosen and purchased expressly for him. Copper was trying to figure out what to write in it. After Copper had read his uncle's notes, his mother had read them as well. When his mother returned the book to Copper, she also gave him this new notebook and suggested that from then on, he, too, could record his own impressions.

Copper had been poring over the new notebook, racking his brain for quite a while now, trying to think of an impression to write in it.

But it turned out that impressions didn't well up naturally, and on top of that, they weren't the sort of thing you could just dream up, even if you tried. Copper had learned lots of things from reading his uncle's notes, but still nothing was coming to mind, other than things his uncle had already thought.

He had all sorts of feelings, but when he tried to write them down, somehow, they wouldn't come together. Before Copper knew it, his thoughts had left the notebook and wandered off toward the kitchen.

In the kitchen, as was her custom during Higan, his mother was hard at work with the maid, making *ohagi*, rice cakes covered with sweet red-bean paste, sesame, and other treats.

Impressions are not something that can be manufactured like rice cakes.

An impression like this came floating into Copper's head, but it wasn't the kind of proverb you could use to start a brand-new notebook. Eventually Copper gave up trying to write an impression and stood up.

He slid open the shoji door, and the weather outside was fine. Splashes of yellow from the daffodils beginning to bloom here and there in the yard were so bright that they made him feel wide awake.

Copper stepped down into the yard and walked around, soaking up the sun.

The maple tree was covered with bright-red buds bursting through the hard bark on all its boughs. On the eight-fingered paper plant, new shoots covered in their thick mantle were poking their heads out like bamboo, while others like tiny jewels graced the narrow tips of the enkianthus. Anywhere you looked in the yard, new growth was everywhere, pushing up the soft soil, swelling the stiff treetops, yearning to get out into the open air.

And faster than all the rest, the blades of grass were peeking up from the ground—as if to say, *Look at us!*— lifting their fresh faces, and stretching with all their might upward.

Copper had a good feeling. Soon enough the time would come to take off his heavy sweater. The crack of the bat, too, echoing across the ball field, was not far off.

Suddenly, under the cypress tree in the corner of the yard, he spotted a mud-encrusted ball. *What*, Copper thought, *the one I lost last fall? I searched everywhere and couldn't find it, and now it turns up right here, just like that.* Copper laughed and picked it up. The ball must have rolled over and spent the whole winter resting there.

When he thought about how many times the snow must have accumulated on top of the ball as it lay there silently, and then how many times it must have melted away again, Copper could really feel how the long, long winter had eventually passed away.

Taking a small shovel out from under the narrow wood porch at the side of the house, Copper transferred some newly sprouted flowering plants from the shade to a spot where the sun could reach them. Although they were the same daffodils, the ones in the sunny places were already in bloom, while the ones where the light was bad weren't even budding.

Copper wandered here and there in the yard, and everywhere he came upon a poor little struggling flower, he transplanted it to a warm place.

"Well, that seems to be all of them," Copper said and looked around. Poking up all alone near where the ball had fallen, an isolated sprout that looked like it might be a flowering plant caught his eye.

"Okay, just one more, over there."

Copper quickly started to dig it up.

But once he started digging, Copper had a surprise. At first he thought it couldn't be more than five centimeters down, but no matter how deep he dug—first five centimeters, then almost ten—the root still wouldn't come out. He worked the shovel carefully down into the earth, digging a hole all around the sprout.

The hole got slowly deeper and larger, and the damp soil piled up little by little at Copper's feet. In the dim hole in the shadow of the great cypress tree, the lonely stem seemed a bit forlorn, stretching upward, pale with just a little green toward the tip. Ten, eleven, twelve centimeters—Copper continued his eager excavation. But still the root wouldn't come out.

When he got past fifteen centimeters, Copper started to get excited. This one little plant, working its way through the soil to the surface from so deep in the earth and bravely lifting its head up toward the sky! In spite of himself, Copper began to admire the little plant.

Even at twenty centimeters, he hadn't reached the end of the root. He gazed in astonishment at the slender, pale stalk. It looked much more like a spring onion than like a flower.

And how many days must it have taken to grow this far? It must have been at least ten or fifteen. When he thought about it, he realized this plant must have known spring was coming soon, even way back when the ground was covered with snow, and slowly, deep under the earth, it had started getting ready to send up a sprout. And then in the darkness of the soil, little by little, it had stretched itself upward without a rest, until just recently, at last, it lifted its face up above the surface of the ground.

What a patient little fellow! Copper's heart called out to it.

Thinking of the little plant silently working alone in the dark with nobody watching it until now, Copper felt something stirring in him. Already this strangely shaped plant had become a figure of some consequence to him.

Well done. Well done! he thought, almost out loud, and eagerly started digging again.

Eventually the root came into view. Copper could see immediately that it was a daffodil bulb. What he couldn't figure out was how a daffodil bulb had found its way into such a deep place.

However, even after being buried so deep in the ground, this bulb hadn't died. And as long as it survived, it still felt the warmth of the sun, even with the heavy blanket of earth covering it, and sent out its shoot as spring drew near, tirelessly reaching up toward the bright surface.

Copper carefully lifted up the strange daffodil. At about a third of a meter long, it was pretty much the same height as its companions blooming here aboveground. But to look at it, nobody would recognize it as a daffodil. The white stem part looked like nothing so much as a spring onion. Only the very crown of the plant, where it was tinted a tiny bit green, resembled a daffodil, and then only if you knew what it was.

Copper carried this funny daffodil over to its colleagues lined up shoulder to shoulder in the sun, and planted it. He dug an extra-deep hole and buried it so that the white part was beneath the ground, as it had been before.

The other daffodils stood there with their deep-yellow flowers half open, spreading their bright-green leaves gracefully into elegant forms, looking just as if they had been washed clean. Looking at the daffodil he had just planted, its head poking up slightly next to the others, Copper felt an irresistible surge of pity and love. That pale stem, hidden in the earth, pushing itself up to be seen by Copper.

That's it! It's because this one couldn't help but grow, even from so far down.

Copper thought about it one more time. The power filling this single bit of green, that need to grow, made this small, humble plant lift up its head proudly, but . . .

But when you lifted your eyes to look around, that need to grow was right now, at this very moment, start-ing to move; it was in the maple, in the paper plant, in the enkianthus—really, in each and every plant in the yard.

Copper forgot to wash the dirt from his hands and stood still in the warm sunlight. His chest swelled with a good feeling.

The same need all those plants felt was stirring inside him as well.

That evening, Copper and his uncle were having a talk in his uncle's study.

It was a quiet evening.

The fragrance of clove flowers drifted in from some-where on the chilly evening air that came flowing through the slightly open window.

". . . But, Uncle, is that story true, that the Greeks were the first ones to make a Buddha?"

"It's true. British and French scholars labored mightily for many years to verify that."

"Are you sure?" Copper made a dissatisfied face.

Copper had come to his uncle's house during the day on an errand for his mother, with the sweet rice cakes she had made, but then his uncle had invited him to stay for dinner, and after eating, they were deep in conversation in the study.

They had started talking about the Higan holiday and then shifted to Buddhist sculpture, and it had become a talk about what statues of the Buddha meant, how old they were, and who had made them.

In the course of the conversation, Copper's uncle had mentioned that the first sculptures of the Buddha had been made two thousand years before, by Greek people. However, that was so unexpected that Copper had trouble believing it. The Greek statues that Copper knew all had streamlined figures, with handsome, well-proportioned faces and graceful arms and legs—they were fine objects that gave him a cool, refreshing feeling when he looked at them.

But when it came to the Buddhist sculptures Copper knew, whether it was the giant Buddha at Kamakura or the one at Nara, they were all pretty chubby, with round faces and heavy closed eyelids, and they appeared to be deep, deep in thought over something. Even though they had infinite benevolence and dignity, from Copper's point of view they were somehow melancholy, and they gave him a mysterious, unearthly feeling.

And neither their faces nor their figures ever seemed at all Western. As a rule, Copper thought, when it came to Eastern things, there was nothing more Eastern than a Buddhist statue.

And in spite of that, to think that the first people to make statues of the Buddha were Greek sculptors making Greek statues . . .

"But, Uncle, Buddhism started in India, didn't it?"

"That's correct. So in terms of the country they came from, the first of those statues did come from India. But even though they were made there, the people who made them were Greek, not Indian."

"Really?"

"Well, have a look at this photograph."

Copper's uncle opened a thick Western book and, turning to an illustration inside, showed it to Copper.

There, several Buddhist statues were displayed alongside a Greek statue.

"What do you think? They look alike, don't they?"

Of course, while one could tell at a glance that the sculptures were Buddhas, their faces had something Western about them, and things like the way the fabric of their clothes folded were strikingly similar to the Greek statue.

"These Buddhas are a little strange, aren't they?" Copper said.

"When you say 'strange,' what exactly do you mean?"

"Because they look like Westerners, somehow."

"Don't they? Isn't it hard to believe that Buddhist sculptures, even ones like these, were made by Westerners? On the other hand, they're different from Greek sculpture in some ways. First, they all have elongated earlobes like this. And then, don't their expressions have something Buddha-like about them, as if they're deep in thought?"

That was certainly so. The Buddhas shown here felt like they belonged in the same groups as both the Greek sculptures and the usual Japanese and Chinese sculptures of the Buddha. Either way there were both similarities and differences.

"Uncle, what's this one called?"

"This is a Gandhara Buddha."

"Gandhara—what's that?"

"Gandhara was a country that existed in the northwest region of India a long time ago . . ."

Copper's uncle told him the story of the Gandhara Buddha.

"You probably know about a country called Afghanistan, bordering India to the northwest. There's a river that flows from Afghanistan into India and drains into the Indus River. This is the Kabul River, and along this river, just after it crosses the border to India, there is a city called Peshawar. Long ago, the land around this city of Peshawar formed a region that was called Gandhara.

"Starting about a hundred years ago, sculptures with a connection to Buddhism were uncovered occasionally here and there in Gandhara, but in 1870, after a British scholar named Leitner took many of these relics back to Great Britain, suddenly the artwork of this area drew the attention of scholars throughout the world. And then many, many Buddhist sculptures were dug up here.

"Originally, Buddhism started in India. About twenty-five hundred years ago, a prince named Siddhārtha Gautama, born in central India, wanted with all his heart to rescue humanity from suffering. For many years, he led a life of hard study and meditation and then began to preach his teachings. He came to be called the Buddha, and his teachings were known as Buddhism.

"After that, Buddhism spread, little by little, and in particular, about two hundred years after the death of Siddhārtha, there was a famous king named Ashoka, in the country of Magadha, who devoted his great power to promoting Buddhism, so Buddhism spread not only throughout India but outside the country as well.

"In this way, for a time, it had extraordinary momentum, but later, it was gradually overwhelmed by the Hindu faith, and after that, followers of Muhammad invaded India and persecuted Buddhists. Eventually India—the land that had given birth to Buddhism—became a place where that religion held nearly no influence at all.

"And then the surviving Buddhist artworks and buildings and monuments were, for the most part, destroyed or buried in the earth, and their locations were eventually forgotten.

"But in the middle of the eighteenth century, India became a British colony. Because the British needed to govern India, they felt they should know India's history, but the Indian people were a mystery to them. Although they had left behind a surprising number of religious texts and things of that sort, there were hardly any surviving written materials about their own history.

"Because there were no historical records, the British had to rely on ancient ruins and remains. The British government had been engaged in large-scale archaeological expeditions and excavations on some of these sites for as long as a hundred years. As a result, a series of ruins, buildings, monuments, artworks, currency, and more were all discovered one after another, all over India, so that now we can accurately know its history.

"And in that process, we also came to a fairly clear understanding of the path of development of Buddhist art.

"The Gandhara Buddhas were discovered through this

kind of research and, as a result of detailed comparative studies, were later recognized as the oldest sculptures of Buddha.

"When people studied these Buddhas, they realized—as you quickly did—that their faces and figures were strikingly similar to those of Western people. Technically speaking, there were points that were exactly like Greek sculpture. Among those was the fact that they had the exact same faces as statues of the Greek god Apollo.

"Still, if that were the only reason, one could imagine that the people of India had simply studied Greek sculptures and re-created them. But in this case, there was another reason to believe that the creators of these statues couldn't possibly have been Indian.

"These Buddhas had their hair tied up in a topknot. In Buddhism, those who take orders and become monks must shave their heads, and it's written clearly in the texts that Siddhārtha Gautama shaved his head, too.

"So if the people who made the Gandhara Buddhas were Indian people, there would have been no need to make the hair tied up like that.

"Although if we're just talking about any kind of Buddhist art, there have been quite a few discoveries older than the Gandhara Buddhas. But among all of those older sculptures, none have been found that show a Buddha in human form. Moreover, it seems that this was not because

Indian sculptors lacked the skill to do such figures, but rather because they deliberately avoided these.

"Among these older sculptures, there are a fair number of human figures other than the Buddha, but the Buddha himself is represented only with symbols such as a tree, a wheel, or a tower.

"The Sanchi Stupa is a world-famous monument built by the Indian king Ashoka of Magadha, whom I mentioned earlier. On the site of the ruins there is a stone gateway that seems to date back to 100 or 150 BC, and even though the life of the Buddha is represented in sculpture on it, there's nothing to be found anywhere on the gate but symbols for the Buddha such as those I just now mentioned.

"So it seems as if, at least until three or four hundred years after Siddhārtha's death, it must have been the custom of the Indian people not to carve images of his form. According to some scholars, this may have been because they thought it sacrilegious to use a human form to represent a divine being.

"And if that's the case, doesn't that make you think all the more that the makers of the Gandhara Buddhas were not Indian people?

"But the expressions on the faces of the Gandhara Buddhas don't look like anything we see in Greek sculpture. The Greek gods have bright, cheerful faces, but these Buddhas have solemn expressions, as if they are deep in thought, and the feeling we get from them is entirely different.

"No matter how much they might resemble Greek sculpture in technique and outer form, the overall mood expressed by these Buddhas couldn't be more Indian, couldn't be more Buddhist.

"If one takes all these points together, one might conclude the following: the people who made the Gandhara Buddhas were Greeks who had spent a fairly long time in the East, soaking up the mood of Buddhism.

"But when it comes down to it, were there actually such Greek people in the area of Gandhara?

"There certainly were. Many ancient coins have been dug up in the area from northwest India to Afghanistan. The coins are from two ancient kingdoms, called Bactria and Greater Yuezhi, which thrived in that area eighteen or nineteen hundred years ago. They feature carvings of Indian gods and Buddhist art, but also of Greek gods, and there are letters from both Indian and Greek alphabets on them.

"When you look at these, it's clear that many Greek people lived in this area.

"So then why did such a great number of Greek people live in northwest India?

"This was the result of a great expedition of Alexander the Great—you may already know something about him.

In 334 BC, this emperor led the allied forces of Greece across a strait called the Hellespont on the border between Europe and Asia, and then spent more than a decade in conquest of the Asian continent.

"Around then, a country called Persia occupied a vast territory, from Syria and Egypt on the Mediterranean Sea in the west, all the way to the area around the Indus River in the east.

"The army of Alexander the Great swept across these Persian lands like a windstorm. They sacked Babylon, the Persian capital in Mesopotamia, and kept going, advancing the army on expeditions from today's Afghanistan in Central Asia all the way to the east bank of the Indus River.

"Alexander ended his Indian campaign in 323 BC and returned to Babylon, establishing it as the capital of the new empire. But that year, unfortunately, the great king died at the young age of thirty-two or thirty-three, still holding on to his youthful ideals.

"Now, about the emperor's ideals—what were they?

"They were to establish one great empire out of all the vast lands that he himself had conquered, blending Eastern civilization and Western civilization together into one.

"Starting with himself, he took a Persian princess for a wife and encouraged his officers to marry Persian women. Also, as he reached important locations during his campaign, he would create Greek towns and have Greek people settle there. In this way, making the Persians more Greek and the Greeks more Persian, he tried to unite East and West.

"The emperor's acts laid an important foundation for the spread of Greek civilization into the Eastern world and allowed it to blend into Eastern civilization. After just over a decade of activity, his life came to an end, but Greek people continued to settle in the East, and for a long while afterward, there was a great exchange possible between the two civilizations of the Eastern and Western worlds.

"Bactria was in the region we now call Afghanistan, and a particularly large number of Greek people were living there. Then, around two thousand years ago, these Greeks gradually began to flow into the northwest part of India.

"They carried the current of Greek culture, while they lived immersed in the Indian civilization. They had knowledge of the Greek sculptural arts, and at the same time, they drank in the religious atmosphere of Buddhism.

"And these people brought the first sculptures of the Buddha into the world."

"And so, Copper," his uncle said after the long story, "the Buddhist art we know doesn't arise from Buddhist ideas alone. Nor was it produced using Greek sculptural techniques alone. It's something that was created by joining the two things together. Until then, even though the Buddhist religion was practiced, there were no Buddhist statues."

From his uncle's explanation, Copper understood that Greeks were the first to produce Buddha statues. Despite that, to think that these Buddhist sculptures, which were so iconic of the East, were actually children of both Eastern and Western civilizations, naturally couldn't help but give him a strange feeling.

"So, Uncle, the Big Buddha at Nara is also like that?"

"That's correct. That huge statue was made by Japanese people, but the skills to do so came from China. And China learned them from India. If you follow them back to the source, you end up at the Gandhara Buddhas again, and from there you are connected all the way to Greek sculpture."

"I guess so," Copper said wonderingly. His uncle continued speaking.

"Starting in Gandhara, Buddhist sculpture was carried along on the tide of Buddhism just as it was spreading throughout Asia. It became familiar everywhere in Asia, and then it reached southeast through Java, and northeast by way of China and Korea to Japan. Along the way, it was influenced by the traits of the people in this or that area, and minor changes arose here and there. But even when they took different forms, the exceptional Greek sculptural techniques were handed down without being lost in the end."

Copper's uncle paused here, and then, changing his tone a little, he went on.

"Now, it turns out that Buddhist sculpture was introduced to Japan during the reign of Emperor Kinmei, in the imperial year 1212. That's roughly sixteen hundred years ago.

"Of course, transportation was not very well developed then. At the time, to travel back and forth between Japan and China, or China and India, was a life-and-death venture! Between China and India in particular, there were great mountain ranges and deserts. What's more, it was a time when you couldn't do much by boat, so you had no choice but to cross these natural barriers.

"Even today, travel through Central Asia from India to China or from China to India isn't easy. So you can imagine what a difficult thing it must have been one or two thousand years ago.

"Copper, imagine these difficulties, and then consider the journey that Buddhist sculpture made before its introduction to Japan. Isn't it a tremendous thing?

" 'Art and knowledge know no borders.'

"Perhaps you've heard these words before? It's just as they say. Neither the great mountain ranges that they call the backbone of the Asian continent—the Himalayas, the Hindu Kush, the Kunlun—nor the great deserts like the Takla Makan were able to prevent the advance of great art.

"When you think of how Greek civilization flowed right over all these natural barriers well over a thousand years ago, crossing the Chinese mainland and carrying as far as distant Japan—Copper, one can't help but be truly surprised, don't you think?"

It was a truly surprising thing. Copper was deeply impressed but didn't know how to put his feelings into words.

"And, Copper, that current didn't just carry Buddhist sculpture. Among the imperial treasures at the Shosoin treasure house at Nara, many artworks have been preserved even to this day from the area around India, Persia, and Afghanistan. The Japanese during the Nara period in the eighth century AD—our own ancestors—didn't know anything about world history or world geography at that time, but still there was no way to cut themselves off from it.

"And then, even though our people were still like children in terms of world history, they admired great things for what they were, and had the spirit to understand their value.

"They had a deep admiration for great things and the artifacts of distant countries, and welcoming these, they steadily enriched Japanese culture. And then the Japanese people, too, advanced the progress of the human race in their Japanese way . . ."

Copper felt like his own eyes were shining.

Such a far, far distance, from Greece to the eastern edge of the Eastern world—two thousand years of time, through the births and deaths of billions of people—

And then, coming into the world here and there, through the hands of the people of all these lands, beautiful culture!

It was a vast and marvelous prospect. A swell of emotion rose within Copper, and the feeling left him trembling. Borne on the evening breeze, the scent of the clove flowers washed over him, and Copper sank into silence for a while and gazed at the table lamp.

The thing he had felt in the garden earlier that day, that thing that needed to grow at all costs, had moved through how many thousands of years of history, getting bigger and bigger?

Chapter Ten

Spring Morning

He awoke from a quiet, dreamless sleep.

It was completely dark in the room. Everyone must have been sleeping still, for there wasn't a sound anywhere.

Copper opened his eyes in the darkness and lay there for a while without moving. He had the peaceful feeling that comes after a deep, uninterrupted sleep.

But what time was it . . . ?

When he looked around, he could see a dim blur of light in the frosted glass of the window, seeping through the gap between the shutters. The night was giving way to dawn.

Copper got out of bed and carefully slid open the window, trying hard not to wake his mother, who was sleeping downstairs. Outside there was a heavy mist. The cool, damp air played lightly over Copper's face as it flowed into the room.

The sun had not yet risen. When he looked out of the second-story window, the trees in the yard, the neighbor's roof, the faraway groves and telephone poles were all enveloped in mist, and in the faint light coming from nowhere in particular, everything still seemed half-asleep.

Then, briefly, from somewhere outside, Copper thought he heard the call of a nightingale. He strained his ears and waited, and after a while, there it was again— another faint, faraway call. Copper couldn't see it, wherever it was. He could only hear its voice, coming through the deep mist. It sounded really happy. It wasn't asking anyone to listen but seemed happy just to sing, enjoying its own voice. Each time it called, Copper could almost see it, imagining the little figure listening intently to its own voice as it disappeared in the distance. Leaning on the windowsill, Copper stood for a while, and he, too, listened.

Before long, Copper sat down at his desk and, taking out his new notebook, started writing steadily with his fountain pen.

Uncle,
- I've decided that from now on I will write my impressions in this notebook. The same way

you wrote your notes as if you were talking to me and wanted me to hear, I'm going to write this as if I'm talking to you.

I went back and read your notes again. There were still parts that were confusing to me, but I didn't give up, and I read them many times.

What moved me the most, naturally, were my father's words. I will never, ever forget that my father's last wish was for me to be a great example of a human being.

I think I have to try to be a truly good person. As you said, I am an expert consumer, and I don't produce anything. Unlike Uragawa, I couldn't produce anything even if I wanted to.

Still, I can become a good person. I can become a good person and create one good person for the world.

And I think that if I can just do that, then I might become a person who can create even more than that.

At this point, Copper stilled his hand and stopped writing. From deep in the mist, there was the sound of a train passing by. They were already starting to run.

Copper looked out the window. The sky in the distance was already getting bright. Under that sky spread the streets of Tokyo. Millions of people would be getting up soon and beginning their day's work.

Uragawa, too, would be rising—no, Uragawa would have risen long before, and just about now he would be standing by the steaming pot, busily preparing the tofu.

In his mind's eye, Copper saw Mizutani's old-fashioned mansion and Katsuko, too.

He could imagine Kitami's sleeping face.

The joy of having good friends came flooding back into Copper's chest. Copper turned back to his notes and continued to write.

> I think there has to come a time when everyone in the world treats each other as if they were good friends. Since humanity has come so far, I think now we will definitely be able to make it to such a place.
>
> So I think I want to become a person who can help that happen.

Suddenly the surroundings brightened, and Copper looked up. Full daylight was streaming through the window. The sun had broken through the haze and begun to throw fresh light on the earth.

Copper came to live his life by this thought. And so this long, long story, for now at least, comes to an end.

And now I think I want to ask all of you a question.

How will you live?

A Note from
the Translator

At first, I thought *How Do You Live?* was just the story of a boy and his uncle. The boy is becoming a young man and has adventures with his friends. The uncle cares for his nephew and offers him advice. A lot of advice. It's funny, sad, and, sometimes, it's beautiful in a particularly Japanese way—how it paints a portrait of the city of Tokyo in 1937, for instance, with its distinct neighborhood land-scapes and tree-lined suburbs, through all the seasons of the year. As I read more of the book, I discovered that, in addition to the story, it contains lessons on everything: art, science, language, history, politics, and philosophy. To understand why, it helps to know a little bit about its author.

Genzaburō Yoshino was born in 1899, grew up in Tokyo, and attended Tokyo Imperial University. He was the son of a successful stockbroker and planned to be a lawyer, but in school his interests shifted. He studied literature and graduated with a degree in philosophy. After graduation he served two years in the army, took a job at the Library of Tokyo, and developed an interest in politics.

During this time Japan was becoming increasingly militaristic and authoritarian. In 1925, Japan passed the Public Security Preservation Law, making it a crime for anyone to say or write things that were critical of the government. A special branch of the police was created—the Tokkō, also known as the "Thought Police." They spied on political groups and arrested thousands of people for their progressive ideas, especially those interested in socialism and communism. Yoshino, who had attended political meetings with socialists, was arrested and imprisoned for eighteen months.

When Yoshino was released from prison, Japan was already engaged in the military campaigns that would lead to its entry into World War II. A friend offered him a job as the editor of a book series for younger readers. Yoshino wanted to write an ethics textbook for this series, to teach the younger generation about the importance of the humanities to society. His friend suggested that he make it a story instead, and so he wrote the novel *How Do You*

Live? For that reason, in addition to being a story of a boy growing up in 1930s Japan, it also contains many lessons, and a quiet but powerful message on the value of thinking for oneself and standing up for others during troubled times. In this respect, it's a unique book, and particularly valuable to us now, when violence against citizens is on the rise, and independent thinkers are being attacked by their governments both here and abroad. In addition to a long and esteemed career as an editor, Yoshino spent much of his life working as an advocate for peace and international cooperation.

I imagine that Yoshino, who was also a translator himself, would share my belief that all translations are collaborative works. This one is no different. This book is special because of the vision of its author, Genzaburō Yoshino, but I also want to thank his estate for placing their trust in Algonquin Books and in this translation to carry his vision overseas. I am grateful to Elisabeth Scharlatt for introducing me to Elise Howard, the skillful, astute, and efficient editor who thought to bring this story into English. Also to friends generous enough to read my English version and help to improve it: Ellen Brinks, Eric Ozawa, Michael and Omara Rosenfeld, Eva Thaddeus, and Akira Yoshimura were particularly helpful in this work. Susan Bernofsky has mentored a generation of translators and I was lucky to have had her advice on this project. My wife, Melissa, and our entire family were constant in their encouragement, and finally, above all, I could not have completed the translation without the careful and tireless help of my father-in-law, Yuichi Ozawa, who spent his childhood in Japan just after Yoshino's book was published, attended Tokyo University himself, and knows from memory many of the places and events described in the book. When I think of how I live, it is thanks to the support of these kind friends.